WHERE THERE'S A WILL

J. A. Newman

ABOUT THE AUTHOR

Coming late in life to creative writing after retiring to Cornwall, 'Where There's a Will' is J. A. Newman's first novel, the seed of which was sown one evening during a creative writing course in 2008.

Following that course, she had her first article accepted for publication in 'Evergreen' in 2010. Since then eight of her articles have been published in either 'Evergreen' or their sister magazine 'This England'. The two Cornish anthologies 'Mining for Words' and 'Write to Remember' each contain one of her historical short stories which were conceived in conjunction with the Caradon Hill Area Heritage Project.

In September 2017 Newman published her memoir 'No One Comes Close' which has been well-received with eleven 5-star reviews to date.

She is now working on her next novel, a historical time-slip adventure set in the Cambridgeshire Fens during the English Civil War, which she hopes to release in 2020.

You can find her on: www.facebook.com/J.A.Newman.author
And on: julieannnewman.wordpress.com

WHERE THERE'S A WILL

Chapter one

'…and now the 9 o'clock news with Jamie Hutchins…'

'Oh my God! Late again. Liz'll kill me.' Jess turned off the radio and dumped her coffee cup in the sink. Grabbing her jacket and handbag she locked the door to her flat and ran downstairs and out the main door, slamming it behind her.

She ignored the 'All right, darlin'?' from a taxi driver, jumped into her bubble-gum pink Ka and joined the stream of traffic. After only a few yards the car in front hit his brakes. Jess blew out a sigh, beeped her horn and pressed the CD button. Beating time to *Material Girl* on the steering wheel she waited for the queue to disperse all the while examining her reflection in the rear view mirror – glossy long blonde hair, perfect make-up accentuating her blue eyes – she was wasted in the back streets of Peckham, stuck in a grotty flat. A shiny penthouse apartment somewhere in Belgravia, or maybe overlooking Hyde Park? Now that would be cool.

As she crawled forward again, a thud and a flash of black jolted her out of her daydream. Jess flung open her door to see what had happened, prompting a cacophony of car horns. She was shocked to see a man had stumbled right in front of her car. Humiliated, he struggled to his feet and hastily brushed the dirt from his overcoat.

'Oh my God. You all right?' asked Jess.

'No thanks to *you*.' He put his weight on his right foot and winced.

She went round to the passenger door. 'Here. Get in.'

'What?'

'Get in!'

She took hold of his arm but he shrugged her off.

More horns beeped. Pedestrians stared from the pavement.

'Look, I'm really sorry, but I'm late for work and I'm holding up the traffic. Either you get in and I'll take you to wherever or...or...I don't know. Please yourself.'

After some hesitation the man slumped into the passenger seat and grappled with his black leather briefcase within the cramped space. She pushed his coat clear of the door and slammed it. The van driver behind shouted a load of abuse and shook his fist at her. Jess gave him a hand signal that wasn't in the Highway Code, got back in the car and began to hum along to Madonna.

Her passenger thrust a finger at the dashboard. 'If you hadn't been listening to that rubbish and concentrating on the road this would never have happened. Can't you turn it down? I bet you were on your phone, too.'

'Huh. Yeah, right.' The car in front moved forward again and stopped. Jess yanked on the hand brake. 'Look, it wasn't my fault, OK? I'm a careful driver. I just took my eyes off the road for a second. What were you doing anyway?'

He didn't answer.

'Where can I drop you? A and E?'

He applied some pressure to his foot. 'No, I'll suffer. Take me to Morgan Bishop.'

'The solicitors'?'

'That's correct.'

'Oh my God, you're not gonna sue me?'

'The thought had crossed my mind,' he glanced sideways at her, 'but no.'

'Phew! You had me worried there for a minute.'

They sat in awkward silence. The man smelled of expensive aftershave and leather. From the edge of her vision Jess thought he looked hot in a well-bred kind of way but ridiculously out of place sitting in her little car.

He looked her up and down. 'Where do you work?'

'Top to Toe. It's a beauty salon.' She noticed him taking sly little peeks at her. 'You OK for time?'

He glanced at his watch. 'I've got a client at nine-thirty.'

'Hang on, be there in two shakes.'

Jess quickly glanced behind, pulled out and screamed down the road narrowly missing a bollard. Her passenger gripped the dashboard as she swerved round the corner and screeched to a halt in Priory Square. 'Here we are then. Bit tricky with all these double yellows. Hope I don't get a ticket.'

He looked relieved to have arrived in one piece and handed her a card from his inside pocket. 'Don't worry, I'm well-connected.'

She scanned it. Giles Morgan. Lawyer. Letters after his name. 'Cool.'

Giles forced a smile, flung open the door and tentatively put his foot to the ground. Jess watched him limp slightly into the Georgian building with a shiny brass plaque on the wall and gold lettering on the windows. Her curiosity was piqued.

Eventually, Jess squeezed into the last parking space at the back of Top to Toe, burst in through the back door and was greeted by the noise and heat of the Monday morning tumble-drier.

'Hiya, Paris.'

The dull junior stopped folding towels and looked round. 'Oh, hi. All right?'

'Not bad. Mandy in?'

'Think she's just gone upstairs.'

'What about Liz?'

'Nah. Popped out for some milk.'

Oops! Jess suddenly remembered she was supposed to buy some on the way to work. Oh, well, another black mark to add to the multitude. Quickly hanging up her jacket and bag in the excuse for a staff room she ran upstairs to the brightly-lit beauty room where she found Mandy sitting at one of the glass-top tables, thumbing through a magazine.

Mandy glanced up. 'Hi, Jess. I was just looking to see what I could do with my hair. You're late. What happened?'

'You'll never guess.'

'Your car broke down? Oh no, that was Saturday. OK... Aidan Turner rang and asked you out?'

'Ha, I wish.'

'I dunno. I give in.'

'Try again.'

Mandy frowned at her and put the magazine down. 'OK so what happened?'

'Nearly ran some guy over, that's all.'

'Blimey, is he all right?'

'Yeah, I think so. He didn't want me to take him to hospital, said he'd be OK so I dropped him at Morgan Bishop. He works there.'

'What? That big flash place in Priory Square?'

'That's the one.'

'Bit ironic – you knock this guy down and he's a solicitor?'

'I didn't knock him down. He fell in front of me car... should've looked where he was going. Anyway, he said he wouldn't dream of suing me and gave me his card.' A cheeky smile crept across her face, eyes wide. 'Giles Morgan. Loaded!'

'Jess! You're awful, that's all you think about.'

'Not quite. Anyway, I might give him a ring. See how he is.'

'You could but I think you're wasting your time.'

'Yeah but... if he didn't want me to get in touch, he wouldn't have given me his card, would he?'

Mandy looked thoughtful, 'He's probably married, anyway.'

'Yeah,' said Jess, screwing up her nose. 'You're probably right.'

Mandy dismissed it and went back to her magazine. 'I'm fed up with boring mahogany. I fancy this berry fruit juice idea. What d'you reckon?'

Jess glanced at the page. The model had reds and purples streaked through her hair. 'Gawd, what would your Trevor say?'

'He won't mind, he likes surprises.'

Jess pulled out a chair opposite Mandy and sat idly flicking through the new nail colour chart. 'I wish I could find someone.'

'Eddie would still love to get back with you, you know.'

Jess reflected on the fact that Eddie didn't share her love of the finer things in life. 'Yeah, but... you know what Eddie's like.'

'Well, I can't blame you for trying, but I don't think Giles Morgan's the way to go.' Mandy took her magazine and ran downstairs to find out if Connie had time to colour her hair.

Jess sauntered over to the large window, looked down into the forecourt and noticed the top of Eddie's fair head as he made his way towards the back door. She ran downstairs and managed to intercept him before he had a chance to walk through to the salon in his oily jeans and a seen-better-days tee shirt.

Eddie's eyes lit up when he saw her. 'Hi, love. Any chance of a whizz-over with the ol' scissors?'

'Eddie! I've told you not to come in here like that. She'll have you strung up.'

'Ol' Liz? She don't mind.'

Jess sighed. 'Look, why don't you come round the flat tonight? I can cut your hair then.' She could cook him a meal too – she doubted if he ate properly these days. Eddie's idea of a balanced diet was a pint in each hand.

Eddie flashed her a cheeky grin. 'Thanks, love. Don't suppose I could cadge a meal as well?'

'You read my mind.'

'Yeah. What time?'

'Make it eight. Give me time to get myself sorted.'

'OK, see you later.' He kissed her on the cheek and left with a spring in his step. She was secretly looking forward to seeing him again but she knew there was no future with Eddie, a car mechanic at his mate Andy's garage on minimum wage. She'd had enough of scrimping and scraping to last her a lifetime.

Taking up her position at reception she checked to see how many clients were booked in. It was a typical boring Monday. Liz had her diehard regulars, one of whom was waiting at reception, and Connie had a couple of cut-and-blow-dries. Apart from that it was dead quiet.

'What did Eddie want?' asked Mandy, searching under the desk for the hair colour chart.

'Oh, just wanted me to cut his hair. I told him to come round tonight.'

Mandy found what she was looking for, nodded. 'So, why don't you do any clients in the shop then, Jess?'

She thought for a while and shrugged. 'I dunno. I'd really like to find a different job, but I dunno what. I don't want to end up like Liz. She's been here since she left school.'

'When was that?'

'Sometime in the eighties, I think. My Nan used to come in here to get her hair shampooed and set when I was little. That's when upstairs was still a wig boutique.'

'Really?'

Jess nodded. 'I used to come in with her, sometimes. I'd sneak upstairs and try all the wigs on.'

'You little devil. What was it like in here, then?'

'Everywhere was red, like walking into hell.'

Mandy's mouth fell open. 'I can't imagine that,' she said, looking around at the slick black and white décor. 'You must've seen a lot of changes?'

Jess nodded. 'Yeah, too many. I bet Paris sticks it out, though.'

Mandy whispered, 'She's away with the fairies most of the time but she means well.'

'I know, right.'

'Did you hear what happened the other day?'

'No. What?'

Mandy checked to make sure Paris was out of earshot and took Jess to one side. 'She asked what happens to all the hair she sweeps up. Liz told her a little man comes in late at night and sits upstairs making it into wigs. She only fell for it!' Jess let out a squeal and clapped a hand to her mouth. Liz burst in through the door, glared at Jess, told her to show her client through and shoved a carton of milk in her hand. Jess immediately pressed her lips together and tried to avoid eye contact with Mandy.

After showing Liz's client to a basin and telling Paris to shampoo, Jess escaped to the staffroom, put the coffee on and took out her mobile and the card Giles Morgan had given her. Hoping she wouldn't be missed, she slipped out the back to get a signal and keyed in the number but was immediately beaten back by clouds of exhaust fumes from an old truck. She'd try again later.

*

Giles Morgan looked at his client from across his antique, leather-topped desk. Dammit, why did women always have to cry in these situations?

He sighed impatiently, 'All right Mrs Baxter, I shall be writing to your husband stating what you are entitled to. If he doesn't contest the writ it should all go through within a couple of months. We can go from there.'

Mrs Baxter broke into a fresh bout of sobs and searched fruitlessly in her handbag for a tissue. Giles reluctantly pushed a box towards her and walked over to the window. There were times when he regretted going into law, he always found it so difficult to empathise with his clients. If it wasn't such a lucrative profession he would put his time and energy into finding something more suited to his temperament. But on reflection, what else could he do? Early retirement seemed very appealing but that was a long way off.

He returned to his client, now clutching a handful of wet tissues, and was relieved to find she had regained a modicum of composure.

'As I said, I'll keep you informed of our progress in due course. Goodbye, Mrs Baxter.'

She dabbed her eyes and stood up. Shaking her clammy hand, he showed her out and called to his receptionist. 'Look after Mrs Baxter, would you, Gloria?'

A very plain little woman with glasses nodded and ushered Mrs Baxter into the reception area.

Giles closed his door and went back to the window. Above the roof-tops a bright blue sky with cauliflower clouds enticed him to drop everything and go sailing on the south coast instead of being stuck in the office dealing with other people's problems. His thoughts drifted back to the woman with the bright pink car this morning. He could picture her on his yacht, maybe cooking up a dish in the galley to tickle his taste-buds. Also, with his fortieth birthday looming, he needed a woman to show off at his yacht club; it had been a long time since he'd had a woman by his side. Yes, she would be an attractive accessory. Lydia wouldn't need to know; the bitch was safely ensconced in France in her designer shop. Or was she? He thought he saw her this morning, that's what had caused that humiliating incident – he was so intent on trying to avoid her that he wasn't watching where he was going.

There was a knock on the door.

'Come!'

Gloria trotted in with a cup of coffee and put it on his desk. 'Here you are, Mr Morgan. The Mercedes garage rang – your car will be ready for collection at five-thirty. Oh, and er…there's a Miss Jessica Harvey on the phone for you…'

'Thank you, Gloria.'

Giles sat down and stared into his coffee cup. Not another stupid woman with problems. Also, what with that ordeal on his way to work and then Mrs. Baxter, he could do with something stronger than coffee. But that would have to wait.

He picked up the phone on his desk and spoke in a monotone. 'Giles Morgan.'

'Oh, hello,' started Jess, in her best telephone voice, 'I just wondered... um...is your foot OK?'

His expression instantly brightened along with his voice.

'Ah, Jessica, is it?'

'Yes, but call me Jess. Everyone does.'

'Well, Jessica, it seems to be absolutely fine, thank you.'

She loved the sound of his smooth, sophisticated voice and tried to think of something else to keep him on the phone. 'I felt awful. I just couldn't believe it...'

'...Quite. Well, I can assure you I've made a full recovery.' He was about to cut her off when he remembered. 'Erm, as a matter of fact...'

'Yes?'

'... I was wondering how to repay you for getting me to work on time.'

'Oh, that's all right. It was nothing.'

'No, no. Let me take you out to lunch.'

'What, today?'

He glanced at his desk diary. 'Erm... no, not today. Can you make it tomorrow?'

'I'd love to. It's my day off.'

He quickly thought where he could take her; somewhere they didn't know him.

'Meet me at Valentino's at one o' clock. Do you know the place?'

'Yes, I think so. Brandon Street, right?'

'That's correct. Till tomorrow then?'

'Yes, see you then.'

Giles replaced the receiver, made a note of the incoming call and took Jessica's number.

Mission accomplished, Jess was beaming. She was replacing her phone in her handbag when she heard Liz marching through the salon towards the staffroom. Jess's smile dropped.

'There you are! Where the hell have you been? I've been looking everywhere. Hurry up, the phone hasn't stopped. I must get back to Mrs Robinson.'

Mrs Robinson was the Mayor's wife, one of Liz's clients from way back when the salon had been equipped with banks of sit-under hairdryers lining the walls. She came in twice a week to have her iron-grey hair shampooed and blow-dried; a real bread-and-butter customer. Liz showed Mrs Robinson the back of her hair in the hand mirror and asked Jess to help her on with her coat. Mrs Robinson raised her eyebrows when she saw Jess pick up a bright yellow mac.

'Oops, sorry. Wrong one!' said Jess, with a smirk. She replaced it with a tweed jacket which Mrs Robinson snatched from her and threw on. She narrowed her eyes at Jess and strode out of the shop.

After taking two more bookings and showing another client through to the salon, Jess was bursting to tell Mandy her news. Jess came up behind Mandy who was sitting with thick, plum-coloured cream on her hair, flicking through *Hello,* and whispered in her ear. 'Here, you'll never guess.'

Mandy glanced at Jess in the mirror and shook her head, slowly, to stop the tint flicking everywhere.

'I'm going to lunch with Giles Morgan tomorrow.'

'You're not! Come and tell me all about it.'

In the couldn't-swing-a-cat staff room, they tried to keep a lid on their excitement hoping Liz couldn't hear them.

CHAPTER TWO

Jess awoke to cats yowling and fighting in the alley, the clatter of wheelie bins being overturned and dogs barking, setting off her landlady's mongrel downstairs. Her bedside clock said 7:35. So much for the lie-in she'd promised herself. Pulling the duvet over her head she tried to go back to sleep but it was useless – two police sirens screamed down the road.

As she regained full consciousness she realised that today she was going to lunch with Giles Morgan. Wow! She hadn't told Eddie. He would only complain about her getting above herself again.

Last night, Eddie had devoured her expertly prepared Chicken Chasseur as if it was his last meal. A couple of glasses of wine later he was annoyed with Jess for refusing to let him stay the night.

'What's the matter? We've had a nice evening, haven't we?'

'Yeah, course... it's just...I'm tired. Got a bit of a headache, that's all. Shouldn't have drunk so much wine.'

'Come on. You know how I feel about you.'

'No, Eddie. I've told you – it's too late for all that.'

'It's never too late. Can't you see?' he softened his voice and gazed pleadingly into her eyes.

'Please, Eddie. If I knew what you had in mind I would never have asked you round tonight.'

'That's bloody nice.'

'Don't be like that. Look, I want us to stay friends.' She took hold of his hand but he pulled it away.

'Don't look at me like that. It only makes me wanna get you into bed.'

To avoid the awkward moment, Jess cleared the little table and took the plates to the kitchen sink. Eddie came up behind her, put his arms round her waist and brushed his lips against her ear.

She tensed and breathed deeply. 'Please, Eddie. Don't do that.'

'Oh, fuck it! What's the use? I'll see you later.'

He had stormed off down the stairs and banged the main door, making her flinch.

But it was no use thinking about that now. Instead, Jess turned her thoughts to Giles Morgan and the kind of house he might live in. One thing for sure, it would be a mansion compared to her little bug hutch. She jumped out of bed, switched on the radio and put two slices of bread in the toaster.

After washing up her breakfast things she scrutinized her clean fresh living space. She felt pleased with her efforts but it needed a lift. Maybe a couple of brightly-coloured cushions would improve it? She'd have a look round the stores after lunch.

She searched through her wardrobe to find something suitable to wear to Valentino's. The name suggested delicious Italian food, not to mention the waiters! Glancing out the window at the weather – people were hurrying along, collars turned up against the wind – she decided on her smart grey mini dress with long sleeves and boat neck, black opaque tights and black killer heels. At the back of the wardrobe she found her black and white tweed coat with the swing back. She held it against herself and looked in the mirror.

That should do it. Booyah!

In the hot refreshing shower Eddie invaded her thoughts again; she pushed him away. This was going to be a day to remember.

Stepping out of the shower she wrapped herself in a big white towel. There was a knock at the door but she ignored it, moisturised her skin and began to dress. After another persistent knock she quickly ran downstairs, her hair still wet.

Eddie stood on the doorstep and thrust a bunch of supermarket flowers at her. 'Just wanted to say sorry for last night, I was out of order.'

She breathed in their scent. 'Mm, lovely. You didn't have to do that.'

Eddie couldn't take his eyes off her. 'Going out?'

'Yeah, just lunch. Nothing special.'

'Look. I am sorry, love… I behaved like a kid. Am I forgiven?'

'Course.'

'Friends?'

'Yeah, friends,' she smiled.

Eddie was hovering from one foot to the other. 'Well? Don't I get a coffee?'

'Yeah, all right then. Quick one.'

He followed her upstairs and into the living room. 'You smell nice.'

Jess giggled nervously. 'Like I said, it's just lunch.... with Mandy from work. I felt like dressing up a bit, that's all.'

'Look love, if you've got a date with some geezer with money, good luck to you. I only hope he makes you happy.' He kissed her on the cheek. 'But we're two peas, you and me.'

*

Giles Morgan sat in the dimly lit, art deco bar in Valentino's, perfectly groomed in an Italian suit and a shirt so white it was practically ultra-violet. Studying the leather-bound wine list he glanced at his watch. He'd give her another ten minutes then he'd give up on the idea.

Jess hurried along Brandon Street as fast as her killer heels would allow, holding onto her hair to stop the wind taking it and hoped Giles Morgan hadn't given up on her.

At last she reached Valentino's with its smart black and silver frontage and tinted windows, took a deep breath and stepped inside. A cute dark-haired waiter greeted her, took her coat and showed her into the bar and placed two menus on the table.

Giles immediately stood to attention and loosened his tie. He wasn't expecting her to look so stunning. He gestured to a chair opposite his. They appeared to have the bar to themselves.

'Sorry I'm late,' started Jess, 'I dunno where the time goes.'

Giles ignored the comment and handed her one of the menus. 'I've taken the liberty of ordering a bottle of the ninety-eight Chianti. I hope you approve?'

'Cool. Pinot Grigio's my favourite, though.'

'Would you rather a bottle of that?'

'No. It's OK. The ninety-eight thing'll be fine.' It came as no surprise that Giles knew all about wines. Already she felt special.

Giles looked up from his menu. 'Well, Jessica, tell me about yourself.'

'Oh, not much to tell, really. I'd rather hear all about you.'

The waiter brought the wine, ceremoniously uncorked the bottle in front of them and poured an inch of the rich red Chianti for Giles to try. He picked it up, smelled it, swirled it gently around, smelled it again and took a sip. Jess sat mesmerised. Giles nodded to the waiter to pour for Jess.

She took a mouthful. 'Mm, lovely.'

She watched Giles take another sip of wine and set the glass down with a twist between finger and thumb. 'Where shall I begin?'

He started to tell her all about the history of Morgan Bishop, the law business that had been in his family for years. She listened attentively and observed everything about Giles Morgan from his sultry brown eyes to his expensive-looking shoes. His mid brown hair was expertly cut and who-the-hell bothered with cuff links these days? Everything about him shouted money.

'Got any hobbies?' she said at last.

His face lit up. 'Oh, yes. I have a yacht moored on the south coast called Sea Witch. My special lady,' he smiled. 'I go whenever I can.'

As he elaborated on the art of sailing, Jess hoped she was nodding in all the right places. He sounded as if he was reading from a tourist leaflet – eleven square miles of water in Chichester harbour, fourteen sailing clubs and over three and a half thousand craft moored. 'The sea can change in an instant – one minute calm as a millpond with the water lapping the bows, the next like a raging torrent.' He fell silent at the thought and stared into his glass, took another sip.

'Sounds lovely,' said Jess, 'I've never been on a boat.'

Giles nearly choked. 'What? Never? Not even on holiday?'

Jess shook her head. She couldn't remember ever going on holiday – her Nan and her Dad had always been too strapped for cash when she was little and since they had died, all her hard-earned money had gone on rent and food, but she couldn't tell Giles that.

Giles was beginning to feel a little uncomfortable. Thankfully the waiter came to take their order. Poised with his pad and pencil, he raised his eyebrows at Jess.

'Oh, I'd like the bolognese, please.'

He wrote it down and looked at Giles. 'And for you, sir?'

'The Chicken Cacciatore thanks. And something while we're waiting?'

'Of course, sir. Bruschetta and olives come as standard.'

Giles nodded. The waiter took the menus and hurried away.

As Jess wasn't volunteering any information about herself Giles took another sip of wine and told her briefly about the yacht club on the Thames that he frequented.

The young Italian waiter showed them to a table for two in an intimate corner where the bread and olives sat ready and waiting. He pulled out the chair for Jess and flipped his large white napkin over his arm and picked up the bottle. 'More wine, signorina?'

'Please.'

'Just leave the bottle, will you?' said Giles impatiently.

Jess took two more mouthfuls of wine and scrutinized the large black and white photos of the silent film actor Rudolf Valentino all along one wall. 'Nice in here, isn't it?'

'Do you take an interest in that kind of thing?'

'What? Décor or old movies?'

'I was thinking more of the décor.'

'Oh, yeah, very much so,' said Jess. She took a piece of the bread, dipped it in the oil and balsamic vinegar and popped it into her mouth.

Giles stabbed an olive and took another gulp of wine. 'Have you had much experience with interior design?'

'Only with me own place. It's nothin' special but I know what I like.' Jess instantly regretted her East End accent that had resurfaced and hoped Giles hadn't been put off.

In another corner sat a family with two young children. The youngest started whinging, rebelling against being strapped in the highchair. The mother plugged a dummy into the child's mouth hoping to pacify her. Giles was relieved to see the waiter bringing their food. He was feeling more uncomfortable by the minute.

'Spaghetti Bolognese for you, signorina?' said the waiter, in his silky, Mediterranean voice. Jess knew he was putting it on for her benefit but averted her eyes. 'And for you, sir…' he put their plates down with an expert flourish, his dark eyes resting suggestively on Jess. 'Any Parmesan, signorina?'

'Mm, please.'

'Ah, I see you like da full works?' he said, with a glint in his eye.

Giles was beginning to regret suggesting Valentino's. The food didn't look up to much either. Sticking his knife into the chicken he hoped it had been properly cooked but he noticed Jess was enjoying her spaghetti, expertly twirling it round her fork. It surprised him. He wasn't expecting that level of etiquette. At least she wouldn't disgrace him at the yacht club dinners.

'How's your spaghetti?' he asked.

'Good, but not as good as mine!'

'Oh, so you like cooking?'

'Oh, yeah. There's nothing I like better than putting on a good spread, as me Nan used to say.'

'Really?'

Jess nodded. 'There's something very satisfying about cooking a meal for someone. It's a sort of love thing, you know?'

He couldn't answer; he didn't know one end of a kitchen from the other. No, he left that sort of thing to Joan, his housekeeper, who had been with him for ten years, and his father before him. He glanced up at Jessica. Once again he could picture her on Sea Witch producing excellent food and stretching out on deck in a skimpy bikini.

They came to the end of their main course. The waiter resurfaced to ask if everything was satisfactory and would they care for any dessert?

'Oh, not for me,' said Jess. 'I couldn't manage another mouthful.'

'Oh? Are you quite sure, signorina? We have some very silky, tasty ice creams. No?'

Jess shook her head. She was very tempted to play along with him but thought better of it.

'Any coffees?' Managing to take his eyes off Jess for a second, the waiter turned to Giles. 'Sir?'

Jess decided on a cappuccino. Giles ordered a scotch since his chauffer was driving.

The waiter lifted an eyebrow at Jess. 'Would you not like a leetle something extra with your coffee?'

'No, thanks,' she said firmly, trying not to laugh.

Giles wanted to swat him like some annoying insect that kept buzzing around. 'What time do you have to get back to work?' he asked Jess.

'Oh, like I said, it's me day off. No rush. Lucky I caught the bus,' she said, with a nod to the wine.

She beamed at him and he made a mental note to highlight Tuesdays in his diary from now on. Now, when would he see her again? Was he ready for another woman in his life? And was it too soon to ask her to his fortieth birthday bash? It was only a fortnight away. He decided to jump in with both feet, very unlike him.

'I was wondering...' he began, then noticed the waiter heading their way with their drinks. Giles glared at him. He set the drinks down without another word.

'Yes?' prompted Jess.

'Er... yes, I was wondering. I'm having a bit of a bash for my fortieth in a couple of weeks. Would you like to come?'

Jess was wide eyed. 'Cool. I'd love to! You don't look forty.'

This remark appealed to his vanity but he shrugged it off. 'Nothing special, just a few friends. It'll be at the yacht club.'

Jess was stunned into silence; it was like a dream come true. She was already planning what to wear.

Giles suggested he give her a ring in the week to make arrangements. However, she was unprepared for his next question.

'Where do you live? Can I get my chauffer to drive you home?'

She shook her head. 'Oh, no, no. That's OK. I've got a bit of shopping to do first.'

'Are you sure?'

'Yes, quite sure, thanks.' Phew! That was a close one – she couldn't let him to know where she lived. Maybe she could talk to Mandy about using her address. She lived at Peckham Rye with a view over the park. Perhaps they could come up with a plan.

Giles suddenly stood up. 'Well, Jessica,' he began, 'I'll be in touch,' and offered his hand.

Jess was surprised but tentatively took it. 'Cool. Thanks for lunch.'

She walked to the front of the restaurant where the waiter immediately appeared out of the shadows. 'Uno momento, signorina. Your coat.' He held it out for her and she shrugged into it. He fussed over her, intimately smoothing his hands over her shoulders. She smiled to herself; she had to give him ten out of ten for trying, but she had a far bigger fish to fry.

*

Giles studied the bill. It was a rip-off. He dropped his credit card on the dish and called to the waiter.

'Everything all right for you, sir?'

'Now you mention it, no, and I didn't like your over-familiarity. I think you know what I mean.'

The waiter gasped and shook his head. 'I'm terribly sorry, sir, it won't happen again.'

Giles felt smug. 'Don't worry. I won't be coming here again.'

*

Browsing the department stores, Jess had imagined being welcomed into Giles Morgan's shiny world with all its glitz and glamour but as she let herself into the scruffy, terraced house she regrettably called home she was immediately brought back to the reality of her own surroundings. Rose, her landlady, was standing on the threshold of her own ground floor flat, dressed in a tea-stained, purple jogging suit covered in dog's hairs. Jess resisted from holding her nose against the putrid smell wafting from inside the flat, while Rose's mongrel waddled out and stood next to her. They both looked at Jess with the same blank stare.

'Your Eddie's been round looking for you,' said Rose, in her flat voice.

'Did he say what he wanted?'

'Nah, just said he'd catch you later.'

Jess escaped upstairs to her sanctuary and shut the door behind her. With a bit of luck Giles Morgan would be her ticket out of here.

CHAPTER THREE

Jess, early to work for once, was eager for Mandy's reaction when she told her about her lunch at Valentino's. Mandy sat in the staff room open-mouthed, listening to everything Jess had to tell her including Giles's wine tasting performance.

'Huh! All that sniffing and swirling! Blimey, wine's for drinking if you ask me.'

'I know, right. I didn't think people really did that except on the telly. The Italian waiter was cute, though. I was tempted to play along with him but I don't think Giles would've been too impressed.'

'So what does this Giles look like then?' Mandy asked.

'OK, he's about five ten I s'pose, not fat but not thin either.' She gazed off into the distance. 'Short brown hair, quite thick, and his eyes are a sort of chocolate brown. Quite heavy eyebrows, now I come to think of it.'

Mandy looked thoughtful. 'What are his hands like?'

'What?'

'His hands. You can tell a lot from a man's hands, Jess.'

She remembered the touch of his hand when they said goodbye. 'Oh, I dunno. I suppose they're a bit like the rest of him, smooth. Why?'

'Well, are they very expressive?'

Jess shrugged. 'I didn't take much notice, but when he shook hands with me...'

'Huh! What?'

'Oh my God. Didn't I tell you? When it was time to go, he stood up and shook my hand and said he'd be in touch.'

Mandy was wide-eyed. 'You're joking? You must have felt more like one of his clients!'

'Yeah, I did, a bit.'

They realised they were being too loud. Any minute now Liz would come marching through the salon telling them to keep it down. Jess opened the door a crack and peered out. Owing to the way the mirrors were positioned, she had a good view of Liz's workstation and the reception area. Thankfully, Liz was deep in conversation with Mrs Robinson with the hair dryer at full pelt. Sarah and Connie both had clients too, helping to drown out the sound of Jess and Mandy's banter.

'And another thing,' went on Jess, 'he insists on calling me Jessica. No one's called me that since I left school. And Dad, of course; he used to call me Jessica when I was a little bugger.'

Mandy smiled and shook her head. 'So when are you seeing him again?'

'Well,' said Jess, 'he's asked me to his fortieth birthday bash at his yacht club in a couple of weeks.'

'Blimey! You must've made an impression.'

'Yeah, but I'm really nervous, Mandy, I've never been anywhere like that. And what the hell do you buy a man who has everything?'

Mandy started giggling again. 'A belly-button brush? Willie-warmer?'

They both fell about, helpless. Paris came in to see what all the fuss was about but Jess shooed her out telling her to go tidy the salon.

Jess closed the door and dabbed her eyes. 'No, seriously, and what do I do about him picking me up? I can't let him see where I live.'

Mandy thought for a moment. 'I know – why don't you come to us? You can give him our address if you like and he can pick you up from there.'

'Can I? Fantastic, but what about your Trevor?'

'He won't mind, and besides, I get to see what this Giles looks like,' she said, with a cunning grin.

Yeah, thought Jess. That would work. She could say she was staying with her sister, or something. Peckham Rye sounded much better than Victoria Villas.

'I'll give you a key and you can let yourself in,' said Mandy, 'unless he takes you back to his place for the night!'

'Yeah, there's a thought.'

The sound of Liz's footsteps shook Jess out of her reverie. She jumped up and opened the staff room door.

'Can you take Mrs Robinson's money, please Jess?'

'Yeah, course.' Jess walked briskly to the reception desk to see Mrs Robinson looking down her nose. 'You'll have to do better than that, you know. You'll be getting the sack.'

Jess turned on her over-sweet smile. She would've liked to tell the old duck to mind her own business but she bit her tongue. She couldn't afford to be out of work. But what if she was married to someone like Giles Morgan...

Jess put the money in the till and helped Mrs Robinson on with her coat.

'I suppose you've put me in the book for Monday? Just check, would you?'

Of course she'd put her in the book, all the way *through* the book. Mrs Robinson just liked to hear the sound of her own voice and all the better if the salon was full of clients.

Jess decided to stay at her post after that. She needed to get on the right side of her boss who kept giving her warning looks, especially as she planned to take advantage of the amenities before the big day. Armed with her good looks, glossy hair and the dress she'd shelled out for yesterday, she would be able to make an entrance fit for a princess.

*

Giles drove his silver S Class saloon into the underground garage, set the alarm, closed the door remotely and took the lift up to his apartment. It was a chilly evening and as he let himself in he thought, not for the first time, how cold and unwelcoming the place was. Lydia's first attempts at interior design were everywhere. It hadn't been touched in years and Giles was reminded of his estranged wife everywhere he looked. Damn the woman! He knew it was a mistake when he'd given her carte blanche to decorate the apartment. She had insisted on dark mahogany everywhere and the whole place reminded him of a funeral parlour. Even their king-size bed resembled a coffin. He crossed the marble floor to the console table, picked up the post and scanned it briefly before hanging his coat on the hall stand. On entering the lounge he noticed Joan had left a roaring fire in the grate. He stood in front of it warming his hands for a while, watching the orange flames crackling and licking up the chimney. His gaze followed the line of the ornately carved fireplace up to the dark oil painting above – a Yorkshire landscape in a heavy gilt frame. He viewed the picture with contempt remembering the row that had ensued – he hadn't been allowed to have his own choice, a picture of a galleon on the high seas. He knew he should have done something about it but the truth was he had lost interest in the apartment and had never got around to the task.

At the prospect of another lonely evening stretching out before him, Giles helped himself to a much needed twelve-year-old malt from the cocktail cabinet and took it over to the wall of windows with a view of the Thames. This was by far the best thing about the apartment and he stood watching some of the craft on the river and the darkening sky beyond. There was a gig with a team of rowers. Giles was mesmerised by the rhythm of their oars dipping in and out of the water. The scotch warmed and relaxed him while he tried to forget the miserable day he'd had at the office. Depressing things like divorce, wills and accident claims had him thinking again about how he could reduce his time at work. He downed his drink, poured himself another and went back to the window. The river scene drew him like a magnet but he couldn't imagine bringing Jessica here; his boathouse on the Solent had much more appeal with its bright, airy lounge and large balcony overlooking the marina. His imagination began to run away with him until he realised he hadn't a clue what she was really like or how she would behave when they were alone together.

He refreshed his drink and sat by the fire in his deep-buttoned brown leather armchair. Again Lydia flashed into his mind. What the hell was he going to do about the woman? He kept putting it off but he knew deep down that one day he would have to divorce her. Neither sets of parents suspected a rift, Giles having managed to keep up the pretence, but he couldn't remember the last time she had shared his bed. He saw very little of her nowadays, most of her time being taken up with her business in France and God knew who she was hobnobbing with at his expense.

His thoughts drifted back to the day when he first met Lydia. His parents had persuaded him to accompany them to a Ladies Day at Ascot. It wasn't really his scene but he had agreed to go at the last minute after being let down on a boating day on the Thames. It turned out to be a bright sunny day and Giles was caught up in the atmosphere. He had even placed a couple of bets, when he had been introduced to Lydia – an attractive young woman with bouncy, dark brown shoulder-length hair, dressed in red with a huge hat to match. Giles was drawn to her infectious laughter and her optimism and they were soon married, but as time went on, her flamboyance and loud voice had the opposite effect of grating on him.

Giles woke up with a start. He was cold. The fire had gone out and he was hungry. He went to summon Joan on the intercom but there was no answer so he went along to the kitchen and was surprised to find it in darkness. Of course – it was Joan's evening off. He switched on the light and flinched at the blast of white that hit him full in the face – Lydia's state-of-the-art kitchen was more like an operating theatre. He blew out a sigh. He'd had too much to drink to drive to his club – it was too short notice to summon his chauffer and he didn't fancy eating on his own in one of the many restaurants in Greenwich Market, so he settled for the ham salad that Joan had left him in the fridge. He put it on a tray with a knife and fork and a napkin, and took it into the lounge. He poured himself another whisky and sat eating the meal at the polished mahogany table, gazing at the changing light over the river. He again wondered what Jessica was doing at this time of night. This was madness. He'd only just met her for God's sake. But the more he thought about her, the more he decided to ask her to his boathouse at the weekend. He smiled imagining the two of them together; she would make him feel young again.

Should he phone Jessica? Was it too soon? What would she think? After ruminating for some time he finally dialled her number.

She answered straight away, giggling. 'All right, Eddie. I'll see you on Saturday night if you promise to behave yourself.'

Giles was stumped for words. He hung up. It was pointless. He would go on his own, forget about her. She wasn't his type anyway. He'd been acting like a bloody love-sick schoolboy these last few days. What the hell had got into him?

Jess spoke to her phone, 'All right. Be like that!' and chucked it on the sofa. But after a few seconds she wondered why Eddie had hung up. Who else could it have been? She checked the last incoming number. 'Oh my God! Giles!' She paced the floor wondering what to do. She could phone him back and tell him Eddie was just a friend, but that sounded lame. Also, it made her seem too eager. No, she was screwed.

She went to the fridge and poured herself a glass of Pinot Grigio, slumped on the sofa, hugged a cushion and tried to put Giles Morgan out of her mind. But then she remembered the Chianti she'd had at Valentino's, the sheer luxury of the smooth red wine, and promised herself a bottle next time she went shopping. Oh hell! It would have to be a cheap imitation. She thumped the cushion. She was just getting used to the idea of being Giles Morgan's girlfriend and all the cool things that went with it – the swirl of parties, exotic holidays, shopping in Harrods, living in a state-of-the-art apartment and best of all, never having to work in Liz's bloody salon again. Oh, well, plenty more big fish in the sea….but where and how to hook such a fish?

She idly opened her laptop, went on the internet and typed in 'Fish'. A dating site popped up. After having a laugh over some of the requests it gave her an idea: what if she opened an account and asked for the type of guy she was looking for? But knowing her luck she would probably get some pervert. She was just about to close the laptop when she saw it: 'UNEXPECTEDLY back on the market! Mature male, tall, attractive, GSOH, seeks attractive fun-loving lady to share the finer things in life.' There was an email contact address.

She thought about it. GSOH – good sense of humour. Yeah, she liked a laugh and a joke, didn't want anyone too serious. And yeah, she was a lady. Awesome! She fitted the bill. She clicked on her emails and set to work.

CHAPTER FOUR

The next day Jess was hoping to get a chance to tell Mandy about Giles's phone call but the shop was buzzing. Connie, Sarah and Tina, who came in at the end of the week, had clients all morning and it was the same upstairs in the beauty room. Jess didn't even stop for coffee. She was showing customers through to the salon and generally looking after them until lunchtime and Liz was still keeping a keen eye on her movements.

At 1o'clock Jess checked she wasn't needed, grabbed a coffee from the staff room and ran upstairs, hoping Mandy had a gap between clients.

Sophia was applying a cucumber facial and Mandy was putting the finishing touches to some nail extensions. She looked up when she heard Jess approach. 'Hi, Jess. All right?'

She sighed. 'I think I've messed up, Mandy.'

'What? Hang on. Give me a minute.'

Mandy's customer stood up and went over to the window to see her new fingernails in daylight. 'Ooh, they're fab! I love 'em. Thanks Mandy. These should stop me from biting me own, right?'

'Yeah,' said Mandy, 'you'll have a job to make an impression on them – they're diamond-hard. Watch your teeth!'

She settled her bill and Mandy took Jess to one side. 'So, wassup?'

'It's all Eddie's fault.'

'Why? What's he done now?'

'He kept phoning, pestering me to go out with him. I thought it was him ringing back. I just blurted out, "all right, I'll see you on Saturday night." Then the phone went dead. Oh my God, Mandy, it was Giles. I've blown it.'

'Yeah, does sound like it, but you never know – he might ring back.'

'Nah, I doubt it. Anyway, I've answered an ad on a dating site. He sounds really hot!'

'Jess! Blimey, you ought to be careful. He could turn out to be a rapist or serial killer or some nut.'

Sophia's client couldn't help overhearing. The cucumber slices slid off her eyes and into her lap as she sat up.

'Yeah, Jess, one of my friends did that. He turned out to be a real weirdo. Stalked her for weeks, she couldn't get rid of him, had to get the Old Bill in the end.'

Sophia's beautifully manicured hands pushed her client gently back down on the couch again. She picked up the cucumber slices and waved them at Jess. 'Here, this is supposed to be a relaxing treatment, you know,' and gave Jess a reprimanding look.

'Yeah, well,' continued the client, 'you can't be too careful, Jess.'

'Look,' said Mandy, 'It's too busy to talk now. I've got another client in a minute,' she lowered her voice, 'Come round to mine tomorrow night, OK? We'll have a girl's night in. Trevor's working late.'

'What's this?' asked Sophia. 'A girl's night in? You two should be out clubbing, shaking your bootie!' She laughed.

'You're joking,' said Jess, 'those places make me feel ancient. I swear some of 'em are only just out of nappies.'

Mandy smiled. 'Saucy Meg's is all right. We could do that one night next week, if you like?'

'Yeah, cool.'

Jess's heart thumped suddenly when she thought she heard Liz rushing upstairs to find her, but luckily it was Mandy's next client. Nonetheless, Jess decided to go downstairs before she was missed.

*

On Friday evening, Jess threw some things in her holdall and drove to Mandy's. As soon as she arrived, Mandy's six-year-old twin girls, Kirsty and Keira came rushing to the door wearing brightly coloured jumpsuits, their black hair in tight cornrows.

'Hello, Auntie Jess!' shouted Keira, jumping up and down.

'Come and see what we've got!' said Kirsty, her velvet brown eyes full of mischief.

Jess dumped her bag in the hall and the twins dragged her to the sofa in the living room where two tiny black and white kittens lay curled up on a cushion.

'Oh,' gasped Jess, 'they're gorgeous.' She bent down to stroke the little fur bundles. One opened his eyes and yawned widely revealing a bright pink tongue. 'What have you called them?'

'Mummy wanted to call mine Bustopher Jones, from *Cats*,' said Kirsty, picking up one of the kittens, 'but that was too much of a mouthful, so we just call him Buster instead.'

'The other one,' said Keira, 'he's mine, I've called him Sylvester. We only got them today.' She held her kitten aloft, his paws outstretched in protest. 'He's the best.'

'No he isn't, mine is,' said Kirsty.

'They're both lovely,' said Jess, trying to dispel an argument.

'Mine's got big blue eyes. Do you want to see them?' asked Kirsty pulling the kitten's eyelids back. He meowed loudly.

'Oh, poor little thing, he's only a baby. You should let him sleep.'

'Talking of which,' said Mandy, 'it's past your bedtime. Go along you two – I'll be up in a minute.'

'Aw! Can Auntie Jess read us a story, then?' asked Kirsty, who still had hold of Buster.

'Not tonight. Off you go. And leave Buster here.'

Jess winked at them. They looked at each other and grudgingly started upstairs then they turned round and smiled at her. She watched them go.

'Cute. You're very lucky, Mandy.'

'Yeah, I know. But they can be little monsters at times.' Mandy moved towards the kitchen. 'Glass of wine?'

'Please. You don't mind if I stay the night, do you?'

'No, course not. Any time.'

Mandy took a bottle out of the fridge, poured two balloon glasses of chilled white wine and handed one to Jess. She noticed the label. 'Mm, Pino. Lovely.' She took a gulp and let out a sigh.

Mandy looked at her. 'Well?'

'Oh I dunno. I 'spose it feels like time's running out.'

'Maybe you're trying too hard. There's someone out there for you, you know.'

'Well, it's not Giles Morgan. Pity really.' Jess followed Mandy back into the living room and they sat on the other sofa so as not to disturb the kittens, now resettled into one ball of fur.

'So you haven't heard any more, then?' said Mandy.

'Nope. Still, I can't wait to find out what this other guy's like, the one from the dating site. Sounds like he's got his own business.'

'Why is it so important you find a rich guy? Eddie loves you, you know. He'd do anything for you. You know what they say… all that glitters…'

Jess had to make Mandy understand. 'Yeah, but you don't know what it was like for me, growing up in that bloody awful council flat, Nan and Dad scrimping and scraping to make ends meet, always having to wear second hand clothes, all the kids making fun of me. I don't want my kids to grow up like that. If I have any.'

'Yeah, kids can be little shits. I'm sorry, I had no idea,' said Mandy kindly.

'Nan used to work in the local launderette and she'd get all excited if someone left their washing behind. It meant more clothes for us.' Jess paused, remembering how hard her grandmother had tried. 'But she was a whiz with the sewing machine. I think that's where I get it from.'

'What about your mum?'

'She died when she had me.'

Mandy didn't know what to say. She couldn't picture growing up without a mum. 'I'm really sorry. Must have been hard.'

'Yeah.'

'And your dad?'

'He worked at the canning factory. He used to come home knackered, stinking of fish. He used to work at the docks before that but he lost his job when they closed down. That was before I was born. I suppose they both worked themselves to death. They both smoked. Only pleasure they had really.' She took another gulp of wine and picked up one of the sunny holiday brochures from the coffee table and started flicking through it. 'We never went on holiday, couldn't afford it. I wanted to go to Paris with the school one year but they couldn't scrape up enough for that either. I had a paper round but that money didn't go very far.' She dropped the brochure back down on the table and looked round at the kittens fast asleep. 'Never had any pets, either, could only just afford to feed ourselves.'

'What about social services?'

'Huh, it went some way towards it but we fell between the cracks. Still, we always had food on the table and we were always clean and tidy,' she said, defending her long-dead grandmother, 'and Nan was very particular, she was always cleaning. You could've eaten your dinner off the kitchen floor.'

Mandy realised she'd touched a raw nerve but she was curious to know more about Jess's family. 'You had a sister, didn't you?'

'Yeah, Shelley, a lot older than me. She used to take me out with her sometimes, in the school holidays.' Jess smiled, remembering the times they'd had together. 'We used to sneak onto a number twelve bus and go into all the big department stores in the West End and pretend we were rich. I remember going into Harrods one day and the store detective chasing us out, telling us never to come back. He thought we were shop-lifting. That's when I swore that one day I'd have enough money to shop in there.' She took another swig of wine.

Mandy had never known the reason behind Jess's aspirations. She had never had a chance to talk to her about the things that mattered; their friendship had only sprung up when Mandy joined Top to Toe a few months ago, but now it was all making sense. She felt a bit awkward for bringing it up. She looked at Jess staring into her wineglass. 'I'm sorry, Jess.'

'Oh, don't be. It's fine.' She looked in the direction of the stairs. 'It's all gone quiet up there.'

'Yeah, I won't be a minute. I'll just pop up and check on them. Help yourself to more wine.'

Jess nodded and cast her eyes over Mandy's living room decorated in retro browns and creams with accents of tangerine. She walked over to Mandy and Trevor's wedding photo – he resembled a young Denzel Washington and Mandy looked stunning in her beautiful ivory wedding gown. They were happy but Mandy had told Jess it had been difficult at first to get Trevor accepted into her all-white family. He had gained their respect through his hard work and determination, had worked his way up from Saturday boy in the local supermarket and was now manager of the store. Two beautiful mixed race children sealed the marriage. They seemed happy with their moderate lifestyle but ever since she could remember, Jess had dreamed of living like a celebrity someday. She noticed a DVD that had been left on the TV unit. She picked it up. Cinderella. Yeah, she could relate to that story.

Mandy bounced back downstairs. 'They really like their dad to tuck 'em in but they've had to make do with me tonight. More wine?' She took Jess's glass to the kitchen to top it up, calling over her shoulder, 'Trevor won't be home till gone ten. We could put a film on.'

'That'd be good, or some music? Shelley's favourite was Madonna – she used to drive poor Nan and Dad ballistic. I still like her music though.'

Mandy realised there was no escaping this conversation and decided to indulge Jess. 'Where's your sister now, then?'

'Shelley always dreamed of back-packing round the world. She got as far as Australia, with her boyfriend, and ended up living there. He wanted her to go on to Japan with him, but she didn't want to so they split up. I haven't seen her for years. I've thought about it, you know, following her. But I never had the money.' She slumped back in the armchair. 'Anyway, I like London. But I'd like it more if I lived somewhere like Kensington or Chelsea...' She twirled a strand of long blonde hair round her fingers.

'There's more to life than money, Jess.'

'Yeah, I know that. I'd like kids some day, too, but if I don't hurry up and find Mr Hot-and-Loaded it ain't gonna happen. That brings me back to the advert. I reckon he's an estate agent.'

'What makes you say that?'

'Unexpectedly back on the market?' smiled Jess.

Mandy joined in. 'I wonder why? Perhaps he's got dry rot, or needs rewiring, or new plumbing!'

'Oh my God! I hope he's not some old duffer looking for a bit on the side!'

They began to relax and Jess had the feeling they were in for a good night.

*

Jess woke up to the sound of Trevor shouting, 'See-you-later,' and banging the front door on his way out. When he had come in last night just after ten, Jess and Mandy were well into the wine and *Bridget Jones's Baby*. Trevor apologised for being anti-social, plonked a kiss full on Mandy's lips and said he'd leave them to it. He had to be up bright and breezy in the morning.

Jess looked at her watch. 7.15. She groaned and snuggled down in the bed.

The twins burst into Jess's room with the kittens.

'Mummy said, would you like some tea?' Keira pulled the duvet back and Jess opened one eye. The two little girls beamed back at her and set the kittens down on the bed. How could she get annoyed with them?

'Oh, go on then. How come you two look so bright-eyed?' She squashed the pillow over her head and peeked out from under it. Kirsty and Keira chuckled and turned to go downstairs. 'And take these two with you!'

They grabbed the kittens and ran downstairs to their mother who had been up and dressed wearing full make-up for the past hour.

Mandy hummed to herself as she prepared the breakfast. It had been good to let Jess open up last night, she thought, something much needed.

The delicious smell of frying bacon shot Jess out of bed. She quickly freshened up in the bathroom and threw some clothes on and ran downstairs. 'Mm, that smells good. I'm always starving after a drink.'

'Me too,' said Mandy.

'Can I do anything?'

'You can pour the tea if you like?'

'Sure.'

The twins were tormenting Buster. He decided he'd had enough and lashed out at Kirsty who went crying to her mum.

'Serves you right. Let me see.' Kirsty held out her hand to reveal a tiny scratch. 'Oh, that's nothing, but you'll know next time.' Mandy gave Kirsty's hand a kiss and started dishing up their breakfast.

Both the twins sat at the table and Mandy put a plate of sausages and eggs in front of each of them and they began to tuck in.

At eight-thirty, after a big fried breakfast all washed down with mugs of tea, Jess and Mandy put the girls in the back of Jess's Ka and they set off to East Dulwich where Mandy's mum lived.

'We love your pink car, Auntie Jess!' yelled Kirsty, bouncing up and down in the back seat. 'Yeah, it's cool,' shouted Keira.

The twins chattered excitedly on the way to Mandy's mum's where Jess dropped them off for the day. She watched from the car as a smartly dressed middle-aged woman opened the door to Mandy, gave her a hug and took the twins into the house.

Mandy came back, sat in the car and belted up. 'They're happy. Mum's really good with 'em.'

Jess nodded. 'Yeah, I bet.'

It was a hectic day at Top to Toe and Jess was kept busy with two weddings booked in along with all the regular clients. She was envious of the pretty brides who spouted off about their designer wedding dresses and their honeymoons in the Seychelles and Antigua. Later, Mandy and Sophia were busy upstairs applying the brides' nail extensions and full make-up. Their other clients mostly chatted about their upcoming holidays to places like Ibiza and Greece and made Jess feel as if she lived in a developing country.

She was thankful when the shop closed at 4 o' clock and was able to drive Mandy back to her mother's to collect the twins who were full of what they had been doing at Grandma's – cutting and sticking, drawing, and baking cup cakes. They bundled it all onto the back seat with them.

'Don't eat any of that till you get home. I don't want you trashing Jess's car,' said Mandy.

'Do you want one of our cakes, Auntie Jess?' asked Keira, hoping this would give them an excuse to help themselves.

'Not right now, thanks. I can't eat while I'm driving. Save it for me.' In the rear-view mirror, Jess noticed the twins pull dissatisfied faces at each other and she smiled to herself.

As Jess parked the car on Mandy's drive she couldn't help noticing the pretty front garden and the tubs of red and yellow tulips that stood at the front door. 'Your garden's nice, Mandy.'

'Thanks. I like pottering about. I've got some more annuals to prick out in the greenhouse tomorrow; there's always something to do.'

'I wouldn't know where to start. I've never even had a window box.'

They had just got through the front door when Jess's phone started beeping. She fished it out of her bag. 'Oh my God. It's Giles!'

Kirsty, who had run into the kitchen and put the cakes on a plate, came back and shoved them under Jess's nose.

'Not now', said Mandy, 'Go and get changed for ballet, you two. Quietly!'

They ran upstairs, chattering.

Jess was all smiles after the call and went to the kitchen to find Mandy. 'He's picking me up from here at six o' clock next Saturday! Oops... is that OK?'

'Course. See? I told you. And?'

'Well, he wanted to pick me up on Friday night and make a weekend of it but,' she said, screwing up her nose, 'I had to tell him I was working on Saturday.'

'He's keen, then.'

'Sounds like it. He was phoning from his boat house. He's got an apartment at Greenwich, too,' she said, wide-eyed, 'and the party's at his yacht club on the Thames.' She pictured the glamorous people in their designer clothes. 'I'll be bricking it.'

'No you won't, you'll be fine. Just got to make sure you look your absolute best. I'll help you. Don't worry.'

The twins came back downstairs looking sheepish – they were still in their clothes.

'I thought I told you to get changed for ballet!' said Mandy. 'We'll be late.'

'Oh, wow!' said Jess, 'you go to ballet?'

They looked at each other and smiled shyly.

'You're so lucky! I was never allowed to go dancing classes when I was a little girl. Show me what you wear.'

They raced back upstairs, noisily opening wardrobe doors and arguing as to who could get changed first.

'You'll have to come round more often,' said Mandy. 'It's always a job to get them there now the novelty's worn off. But Chris Wheeler's very good with them, and she puts on a little show every year in the town hall.'

'Awesome. I'd love to see it. Let me know when.'

'Will do.'

Kirsty was first downstairs with Keira hard on her heels, both dressed in bright pink leotards and pale pink tights. They asked Mandy to fasten their little net ballet skirts, the same colour as their leotards, round their waists.

'Oh, cool,' said Jess. 'Show me what you do.'

They held hands and went into the middle of the living room. Jess watched as they began to go through their positions, pointing their toes, and decided that if she ever had a daughter and if she could afford it, she'd definitely send her to ballet lessons.

CHAPTER FIVE

After washing up her dinner things, Jess curled up on the sofa with her new copy of *Ideal Home* magazine. The colours and tones advertised were just what she needed to brighten up her living area but she couldn't afford the big name brands, so she pulled out her Wilko paint chart from under the pile of magazines on the floor and decided one of the light neutrals would be perfect. She doubted Rose would have any objection – she never came upstairs to see how Jess was living. As long as she paid her rent that's all Rose was worried about. *Money for old rope* came to mind, one of her Nan's favourite sayings, but it was difficult to find accommodation that she could afford and Jess had settled for making do. She had tried really hard to make her cramped living space attractive even though it was a dump. Eddie had often asked her to move out to the country with him, but Jess wanted to stay in London amongst the buzz and the nightlife. She looked at the window and decided that could do with a lift too. She'd look in the charity shops tomorrow for a remnant of material, something bright and cheerful, and use her Nan's old Singer sewing machine to make some new curtains. Yes, she could picture it all in her mind's eye.

Her phone beeped. She went hunting for it, but by the time she found it under one of the cushions, it had stopped. She listened to the voicemail – "Chris Jenkins, here. You answered my request on the Fish dating site? Can you call me back? Thanks."

She was in two minds. Now Giles had asked her to his fortieth, she wondered if she need bother with Chris Jenkins, whoever he was. But on second thoughts, it wouldn't hurt to have another option on the backburner just in case it all went tits-up again. She rang the number.

He answered straight away. 'Chris Jenkins.'

'Oh, hi. Jess Harvey. You just tried to phone me?'

'Ah, yes. Hello, Jess. I got your email and wondered if you'd like to meet me one evening this week?'

'Cool.'

'Have you ever done anything like this before?'

'Huh, no! Never.'

'Really? Well I have and it actually seems to work quite well. It's quite safe as long as you follow the rules.'

Rules? What rules? She hadn't noticed anything about rules on the site. He told her they were to exchange car details – colour and registration number – and she was to meet him in the car park of The George Hotel.

'Well, you won't be able to miss my bright pink Ka. It stands out a mile!'

'Do you match up to your car?' he asked, with a smile in his voice.

'I like to think so.'

'OK, shall we say seven-thirty on Thursday?'

'Great. See you then.'

Not till Thursday and it was only Monday. Maybe he was overrun with replies? She poured herself a glass of wine and tried to imagine what he looked like – he hadn't submitted a photo or a video. Those spaces had been left blank. Oh dear, it had been silly to reply now she thought about it.

She was suddenly alerted to the sound of breaking glass – a bunch of youths had set off a car alarm down the road. She looked out the window to check it wasn't hers. No. She whistled through her teeth and went back to her magazine. Pointless trying to improve her flat with all that going on in the area but as long as she had a bright and cosy living space she could close her door and temporarily forget where she was. Nonetheless, she fully believed she would come down one morning to find her treasured Ka propped up on bricks.

*

Jess arrived at The George in good time and scanned the car park for Chris Jenkins' red car. It wasn't there. She waited. To while away the time she put *Duran Duran's Greatest Hits* in the CD player, another of her sister's old favourites. Jess felt a pang of envy for her sister's lifestyle and a little sad at the way her she'd been left behind.

She wondered, not for the first time, what her sister's life was really like. Shelley was no letter-writer – Jess was lucky if she got a birthday or Christmas card from her but it didn't matter. Jess knew that when or *if* they ever met up again they would carry on where they left off. It would be like old times. They had tried to Skype once or twice but owing to the poor connection at Jess's end they had given up.

A tap on the window made her jump. She turned to see a man with a beard and glasses peering in at her. Oh my God! Was this him? She turned off her music and got out to meet him.

He offered his hand and smiled. 'Hello, Jess. Chris Jenkins. Sorry I'm late. Bit of a problem at work I'm afraid. Shall we go in?'

As they walked through the porch of the old coaching inn she noticed he was certainly tall but looked a lot older than his advert implied. The thought struck her to turn tail and run, but at that precise moment he turned round and held open the door for her.

They chose a table for two by a small-paned window overlooking the courtyard. He asked what she would like to drink. She would have loved a glass of wine but settled for a J2O as she was driving.

Jess watched him stoop to mind his head on the dark oak beams on his way to the bar. He had the appearance of one of her old teachers at secondary school – a tweed sports jacket and grey trousers – and her heart sank. His height was his only attribute as far as she could make out. *So much for Mr Hot-and-Loaded.* She glanced around the bar in case she knew anyone; she would never be able to live this down if she was spotted, but she was in the clear.

Chris came back with their drinks, sat down and proceeded to tell Jess that he was indeed an estate agent and that Jenkins & Co. was his own business. He had three offices. She thought in terms of estate agent speak, 'an interesting older property in need of some modernisation.' Mandy would find that hilarious! She felt a smile coming on and hoped he couldn't read her mind.

'So, Jess,' he gulped a mouthful of beer, the foam clinging to his top lip. 'What sort of business are you in?'

She decided to play a game and asked him if he would like to guess.

'Well,' he smiled, looking her up and down, 'You're certainly well turned out. My guess is that you're something to do with fashion. Am I right?'

Jess gave him a wide smile and nodded.

'Model?'

'Nope.'

'Designer?'

'Huh, I wish.'

'I give in.'

'Receptionist at Top to Toe. It's a hair and beauty salon.'

Chris nodded. 'My son's got a salon. Razor Sharp. Do you know it?'

Jess nodded. She had seen it but she'd never ventured inside.

'And do you enjoy your job?'

'Not as much as I used to.'

'Oh? Why's that?'

'It's boring; I think I've been there too long. I'd like to find something I can get me teeth into, more of a challenge, you know?'

Chris stroked his beard thoughtfully. 'Am I right in thinking you have an interest in property and interior design?'

'Yeah, how d'you guess?'

'I think you said as much in your email.'

Of course. She could feel her face colouring and regretted not having that glass of wine. 'I've always been into interior design. I take a great interest in me own place – I'm always looking for new ways to make it more visually appealing.'

'Do know anything about selling property?'

Jess shook her head. 'Not much.'

'Would you like to learn? Helping clients to find the right property can be very rewarding, you know.'

She sat back in her chair and looked at him. 'Yeah, I think I would now you come to mention it.'

'Not only will you help them by finding a property that matches their criteria, you can also advise them on how to make their own home more appealing to prospective buyers, enabling them to achieve the best possible selling price.'

'Cool.' She was always watching programmes like that. She knew exactly what he was on about. 'You mean make-overs and stuff like that?'

Chris nodded and took another mouthful of beer. 'Well, it so happens I have a vacancy for a sales negotiator at my, or should I say *your* local branch of Jenkins & Co. Would you be interested?'

'Do you think I'd be any good?'

She could see he was giving this some thought as he drank deeply from his glass.

'You could give it a try, nothing ventured.... you'll need to go out with me and see what it entails. Take notes etcetera. How does that sound?'

'Great. You mean I get to 'try before I buy'?'

'Exactly! Couldn't have put it better myself.'

She smiled smugly and took another sip of her juice.

'When are you free? Your day off, perhaps?' asked Chris.

'Yeah. That's Tuesday.'

'I'll have a look, but I think next Tuesday's fine.' He took out his diary from his breast pocked and studied it. 'Yes, that would be perfect.'

He went on to tell Jess what remuneration she could expect. She tried not to let her surprise show – it was far more than Liz was paying her and he mentioned a clothing allowance. Awesome!

They finished their drinks and arranged to meet next Tuesday morning at 9 am at the office. Chris shook her hand. 'Nice meeting you, Jess. I don't think either of us came out tonight with this intention but I hope you're not too disappointed?'

'Not at all.'

Whilst driving home, Jess went over what Chris had talked about and couldn't believe her luck. A better job and more money and, hopefully, no more fussy old ducks like Mrs Robinson.

*

The next day at work, Jess checked she wasn't needed and ran upstairs to tell Mandy all about her meeting with Chris Jenkins. Mandy was preparing the beauty treatments for the day and checking the stock.

'Oh, hi Jess. How'd it go last night?'

'Great! I've got a new job.'

Mandy looked sideways at her. 'What? I thought you went on a blind date?'

'I did, but he turned out to be 'an interesting older property in need of modernisation', she said in her exaggerated voice.

Mandy burst out laughing. 'So, what happened? Tell all – what did he look like?'

'Well, he was certainly tall but that was the only thing about him that matched up to his advert. I couldn't believe it when he tapped on my car window. He had a beard and glasses and the bit of hair he did have was going grey.'

'Oh? Needs a new thatch, then! How old do you think he is?'

'I dunno, but he looks a lot older than Giles, that's for sure.'

'Dirty old pervert. I told you to be careful, Jess. I bet he does this on a regular basis just so he can get off with younger women.'

'He's all right. Anyway, we got onto the subject of work, of all things, and I told him I wasn't very happy in me job.'

'Really?' Mandy put her hands on her hips and her head on one side. 'So he offered you what, exactly?'

'A job as sales negotiator for the local branch of Jenkins & Co. I'm going out with him next Tuesday to see what it entails.' She smiled at Mandy's disapproving look. 'It'll be fine. I'm meeting him at the office at nine in the morning.'

'Mm. I donno. I still think you ought to be careful.'

'I told you. I'll be fine. And if I do well, I might be able to get a better flat. He's going to pay me loads more than Liz. And a clothing allowance.'

'Yeah? Sounds OK, I s'pose.' Mandy was beginning to warm to the idea. Jess certainly needed to get out of that grotty flat and a better job would be one way of achieving it. 'Well, all you can do is give it a try.'

'Exactly,' said Jess. 'And you never know – I might meet Mr Hot-and-Loaded trying to sell his mansion!'

CHAPTER SIX

At 4:30 Saturday afternoon, Mandy was feeding Buster and Sylvester in the kitchen when there was a knock at the door. She quickly washed her hands and went to let Jess in with her bags and noticed the special evening dress draped over her arm.

'Here, let me help you. Gosh! This looks impressive,' said Mandy.

'Yeah. Cost me an arm and a leg. Still, if it works...'

On her day off Jess had blown her entire week's wages on a slinky little pale blue number with a split hemline and shoe-string straps. She chose her silver strappy heels and her fake silver jewellery to complete the outfit.

Mandy laid her dress out on the spare bed and noticed Jess looked a bit flustered. 'Everything all right?'

'Yeah, think so.'

'You'll be fine. There's plenty of hot water if you wanna bath... I'll even treat you to a massage, if you like?'

'I might take you up on that.' Jess moved her dress carefully to one side and slumped back on the bed. 'I'm knackered – Eddie came round as I was leaving, asked if he could give me car an MOT in the week. I thought he'd never go. I was so frightened I was gonna be late.'

'Did he ask where you were going?'

'Yeah. I said I was going out with you and staying the night,' she looked at Mandy. 'I know it's a porky but it's not that far from the truth, is it?'

Mandy shook her head. 'That's up to you.' She left Jess to get organised and went back downstairs. The twins were excited about Auntie Jess coming to stay again and Mandy had to tell them to leave her alone and let her get ready. She put their favourite *101 Dalmatians* DVD on for them and they sat watching it   until Jess came downstairs wearing a pair of skinny blue jeans, a figure-hugging white top and silver sequin sandals on her feet.

'Auntie Jess! Auntie Jess!' they both shouted.

'You look nice,' said Kirsty.

'You smell nice, too,' said Keira.

'Thanks, you two,' she said, hugging them to her. 'Here, I've got something for you.' She went to her holdall and produced a bag of chocolate muffins. 'I made them last night.'

'Ooh, thank you,' said the twins, their eyes nearly popping out of their heads.

'Put them in the kitchen – you can have them later.' Mandy turned to Jess, 'You shouldn't have done that, you know.'

'It's OK, I enjoyed doing it.'

'Do you want to play a game with us?' asked Kirsty.

'Aw, another time. I've got to go out soon.' They hung their heads, mouths downturned but Jess promised that next time she would have much more time with them.

'We love you, Auntie Jess.'

'I love you, too. Both of you.' She sat between them on the sofa and cuddled them while they watched the film. Mandy was making a pudding for their evening meal and with the homely sounds coming from the kitchen, Jess began to doze.

A loud knock at the door suddenly threw them into a panic, even the kittens started running around like wild things.

'Can you get that, Jess?' shouted Mandy, her hands in flour.

Jess jumped up and went to the door. Mandy heard her say, 'I'll be out in a minute.' Jess quickly ran upstairs to collect her clothes and down again shouting, 'See you, Mandy.'

'Yeah, have a lovely time,' Mandy shouted back but only managed to catch a glimpse of the flash silver car as it drove away.

Jess sat in the back of the Mercedes feeling like royalty – Giles had sent his chauffeur to pick her up. She smiled and hugged herself remembering his words when she opened the door. 'Miss Harvey? Mr Morgan has asked me to escort you to his apartment.'

The interior of the car flooded her senses – blue leather seats and carpet to match. Such luxury! She glanced at the back of the chauffeur's head and shoulders – no uniform but he was very clean-cut, dressed in a smart grey suit and white shirt. He kept his eyes on the road even though she stared at him in the rear view mirror. There was no conversation between them – Jess was quick to realise he wasn't supposed to talk to her. As the car purred along she gazed out the window at the familiar shabby sights morphing into unexplored territory and felt a little anxious about what the evening held in store.

The Mercedes drew up outside a stone building then turned down to an underground area. Jess watched as the garage door opened automatically allowing the chauffeur to park the car inside. After closing the garage again with a flick of a switch he offered to carry Jess's holdall and dress into the lift. This seemed a bit over-the-top but she supposed that's what chauffeurs did. He punched in a number on the keypad entry and escorted her silently up to the third floor.

The chauffeur opened the door to Giles's apartment and Jess stood gobsmacked at the marble floor, the dark wood panelling and the two huge brass lanterns suspended from the high ceiling.

'This way, Miss.' The chauffeur led her into a large bedroom sumptuously decorated in dark reds and purples where he left her holdall and placed her dress carefully on the bed. 'If you'd like to freshen up in the en-suite I'll tell Mr. Morgan you're here. He'll be in the lounge when you're ready, second door on the left.'

'Thanks.'

Jess wondered who had chosen the furnishings for this room. It was all a bit old-fashioned for her taste. In the en-suite, all shiny marble and white with gold taps, some toiletries had been left on the glass shelf, for her convenience she supposed. She picked them up and examined them. Blimey! They all had Harrods labels.

Giles poured himself another glass of single malt and sat on the edge of his armchair waiting for Jessica to make an appearance. He was having misgivings about the evening; he would much rather have been sailing on the south coast and to hell with all this palaver but it had been taken out of his hands, all the preparations having been made by his mother. He hadn't told his parents about Jessica. He was planning to introduce her this evening but he was now feeling apprehensive about the whole thing.

There was a little tap at the door and Giles immediately jumped up to greet Jess and show her in. The sight of her took him aback – her tight blue jeans and short white top showed off her trim figure and pale gold skin to perfection. There was an aroma of expensive perfume too, which surprised him.

'Yes, er, have a seat, Jessica.'

'Thanks.'

She tried not to show her surprise – the room was big enough to house her whole flat. Sinking into the big, squishy dark green sofa, she noticed a large oil painting above the fireplace. For some reason she couldn't take her eyes off it. The light shone onto the dark shiny surface making it difficult to pick out any of the details, but she remembered her Nan saying something about a painting, way back in the family, that went missing.

Giles shook her out of her reverie. 'What can I get you?'

'Oh, d'you know what? I'd murder for a cup of tea!'

He spoke into an intercom and asked Joan to bring a pot of tea for two into the lounge.

Oh my God, servants!

Jess knew she would have to be on her best behaviour. She glanced at Giles dressed smartly casual but with no compromise on quality, and hoped he wasn't scrutinising her bargains too closely. But in fact he had hardly noticed her and she felt a bit disappointed. He seemed preoccupied.

There was a knock at the door. Giles opened it to reveal a little woman with short grey hair and glasses holding a laden tea tray.

Giles went to relieve her of it but she was too quick for him. 'Ah, thank you Joan. Leave it on the coffee table, would you?'

'Of course, sir. I took the liberty of adding two slices of my best Victoria sponge. I thought the lady might be hungry.'

Joan set the tray down and Jess noticed the fancy porcelain teapot, cups and saucers, milk jug and sugar bowl.

'Will that be all, sir?'

'Yes. Thank you, Joan.'

She gave Jess a lop-sided smile and pulled at her fluffy mauve cardigan. 'My Stan always loved my Victoria sponge, bless him. Still, Mr Giles appreciates my baking now, don't you, sir?'

Giles nodded.

'And Mr Jacob before him...' she picked up the vibe from Giles and said hastily, 'well, I'll be off then. I'm baby-sitting tonight.' She toddled off and closed the door behind her.

Jess found it amusing to hear herself called *the lady*. 'Shall I be Mum?'

Giles had moved over to the window and was gazing out. He turned back to her. 'Oh, er, yes of course,' and smiled for the first time.

Jess asked if he took milk and sugar.

'Just a little milk, thanks.'

Jess wanted to lighten up the mood by saying, 'Sweet enough, eh?' but bit her tongue. This was all rather formal and she wondered if this was how he always behaved. She began to pour the tea into cups that looked like Wedgewood but she didn't dare examine them too closely. She instinctively knew that would be a mistake. She picked up a plate, a serviette and a silver cake fork and helped herself to a piece of cake.

'Mm, this is good,' she said, taking a mouthful.

He had remembered her remark in the restaurant, and smiled smugly. 'But don't tell me….not as good as yours?'

'Oh, yeah. Right!'

Apart from these few words they ate their cake and drank their tea in silence until Giles blurted out, 'It was very good of you to come tonight.'

'Oh, I nearly forgot. Here.' She pulled out from her handbag the fortieth birthday card that had caused her so much trouble to find. He set his plate down and took the card to the leather-top desk and opened it with a letter knife. There was a picture of a yacht in full sail on the front. He smiled and looked inside. To Giles, Happy 40th love Jessica. x.

She had decided not to buy him a present knowing she couldn't match up to his expectations. 'I didn't know what to buy you so I'm gonna cook you a special meal here in your apartment. You decide when.'

'Are you sure? You don't have to go to all that trouble.'

'It's no trouble. I like cooking, remember?'

Giles stood the card up on the mantelpiece, picked up his drink and walked back to the windows that spanned the length of the wall and reached from floor to ceiling. Jess went and stood beside him. 'What's so interesting out there?'

He looked surprised to see her standing next him. 'Look out there and tell me what you see, Jessica.'

She couldn't get used to him using her by full name but she ignored it. 'Well, there's the river for one thing...'

'Exactly. It's always changing, do you see?'

She nodded. She supposed these yachting types were like that. She would have to make a point of remembering to notice in future even though she couldn't see what all the fuss was about. To her, there was nothing very exciting about the muddy river Thames, especially at low tide. There was another awkward silence until finally she looked at her watch. 'What time's the party?'

'We'll get there about eight. You should have plenty of time to change.'

'Oh! I was planning to go like this,' she said, her arms splayed out in a pose.

Giles looked crestfallen.

'Joke!' she blurted, with a cheeky grin. Bloody hell, this was hard work. Where was his sense of humour?

'Oh, yes, of course,' he managed a weak smile. 'As I said, take your time.'

She guessed that was her cue to leave – dismissed – so she made her way back to the guest room.

After making full use of the luxurious facilities and putting the finishing touches to her make-up, Jess studied herself in the cheval mirror. A big smile spread across her face; she looked good and felt confident she'd be able to mix it with the best of them this evening. She was about to go back to the lounge when one of her sandals felt a bit loose and as she leant against the wardrobe to tighten the strap, the door creaked ominously open revealing a rail full of women's clothes in fiery colours. She examined the labels; just as she'd thought – designer. But who did they belong to? Certainly not Joan. Giles wasn't wearing a ring but that didn't mean anything. There was obviously another woman in his life but she wondered where she was tonight.

Back in the lounge, Giles was looking at his watch and pacing the floor when he turned to see Jessica looking as if someone had waved a magic wand. He couldn't take his eyes off her. 'Excellent. Shall we go?'

The chauffeur opened the car door for Jess and she sat in the back arranging her dress on the blue leather seat. Giles expressed a quiet, 'Thank you, Benson,' as he too sat in the back the other side but Jess noticed how the armrest sat strategically between them. She caught Giles glancing surreptitiously at her like he did on that first morning and she smiled to herself.

After a short drive they came to the yacht club with its Georgian façade and wrought iron railings. Giles dismissed Benson and escorted Jess through the foyer and into the large ballroom with and a view over the Thames. Some heads turned in their direction then a very loud man in a striped blazer came up to him.

'Giles, old boy,' he eyed Jess up and down, 'I say. Aren't you going to introduce me?'

He winked at Jess who took an instant dislike to him.

'Dickie! Glad you could make it.'

'So who have we here, then?' said Dickie, with a lecherous grin.

'This is Jessica. My escort for the evening,' said Giles.

Dickie gave Giles a nudge and a wink and cleared his throat. 'The usual, Giles?' Dickie moved over to the bar and Giles followed. Another man came over to join them and all three stood laughing and joking. Jess felt abandoned until a waitress came past with a tray of champagne. She took a flute, downed it, and grabbed another.

Giles came back. 'I've got a bit of business to attend to, I hope you don't mind. I'm sure you'll be able to mingle. I won't be long.' Without waiting for her to answer he strode off back to the bar. How rude and how the hell was she supposed to mingle in company such as this?

Before long, Giles was in the middle of a crowd of his cronies all behaving like a load of schoolboys. This wasn't what Jess had in mind; she felt uncomfortable standing in the middle of the room full of people, on her own. There was no one she could talk to – the other guests were all engaged in conversation, in groups. She tried to edge her way into Giles's company but heard some rather vulgar expressions coming from Dickie. He was referring to some antics they got up to behind the bike sheds at school, of all things. 'Ha, yah, Yo-Yo drawers… can't remember her name… I think we all practised on her, didn't we, Giles? Well, don't want to ruin a good one, eh?'

Jess had a name for him – Dickie Dirt, a stuffed shirt. They all were. Not a genuine one among them. If she'd brought her own car she would be out of here and no mistake.

Suddenly, a loud commotion coming from the foyer had everyone turning to see a woman dressed like Cruella De Vil, rushing towards Giles in a cloud of sickly perfume.

'Hello, darling! Surprise, surprise! Just popped in to wish you a happy fortieth and all that. Mummy and Daddy send their regards…' Lydia made a show of affection with a glancing blow of a kiss but stopped in mid flow when she noticed Jess at his elbow.

'Oh! And what have we here?' She slowly scrutinized Jess, lifted an eyebrow. 'He's no good with women, my dear,' she blurted out for all to hear, 'you'll soon learn. We're just accessories to him. Isn't that right, Giles?'

Deathly silence fell on the room. People started talking in hushed tones. Jess looked at them, then at Giles, and flew out of the room.

'Oh! Your little skivvy has run off! Anyway, can't stay. Just thought I'd prove I was still alive. Au revoir!' She was gone in a swirl of red and black with everyone staring after her.

Giles looked decidedly uncomfortable. Dickie came to his aid, 'Ha, women, eh? Have another drink, old boy. Forget it, I should.'

Giles took a deep breath and pushed a hand through his hair. He scanned the room for Jessica. Realising she wasn't there he rushed outside to find her.

Jess had escaped to the ladies loo to phone for a taxi but she couldn't get a signal. She sneaked outside to try again but without any warning, the sky suddenly darkened and the rain came down in sheets. She stood drenched and shivering, still trying to get a signal. She didn't know what to do. She didn't want to go back inside looking like a drowned princess.

A taxi drew up with some late arrivals. Jess snatched her chance and ran to the driver's window. 'Can you take me to Peckham?'

'Yeah, hop in, love.'

Relieved to get away and into the dry she settled herself in the back seat. Not as plush as the Merc but who cared at this moment in time. With the lull of the windscreen wipers and the warmth of the cab she began to relax.

Back at the yacht club, Giles was still searching for Jessica. He'd looked everywhere.

A woman came up to him in the foyer. 'Looking for someone?'

'Yes, a blonde woman in a pale blue dress.'

'Oh, you've just missed her – she got in a taxi.'

'Shit! Sorry. Did she say where she was going?'

She frowned. 'I'm not sure but it sounded like Peckham.'

Jess let herself in and Mandy came rushing to the door. 'Oh my God! I didn't expect you this early. What happened?'

'The Bitch from Hell, that's what happened.'

'What? Who?'

'I'll tell you later. I'm freezing and me hair's still dripping.'

'I'll make you a cuppa. Have you eaten?'

'Nah, didn't get that far. I'm famished. Had a bit of cake about two hours ago.'

Mandy didn't ask. 'OK. Go and dry off, have a bath, whatever, and I'll sort you out something to eat.' Jess made her way upstairs. Mandy called to her, 'You can wear me dressing gown...on the back of the door, and me hairdryer's on the dressing table. Help yourself.'

CHAPTER SEVEN

Giles spent Sunday in quiet contemplation. He strolled down to the river hoping to clear his head. He needed to do something about Lydia once and for all; he couldn't have her humiliating him in public any more. And at his club, too. She did it on purpose, of course, spiteful bitch. Did she hate him that much? What had he ever done to make her so bitter? Thank God they didn't have children. Giles had seen, all too often, the mess people got themselves into with divorce and residence orders. At least he'd been spared that.

Last night, he had fully intended to ask Jessica to his boathouse next weekend but he didn't get a chance. When he returned home last night after the celebrations, something had made him go into the guest room and there on the bed was a holdall containing her clothes. He didn't know what made him do it but he picked up the white top remembering how it had skimmed her curves, held it to his face and breathed in her heady scent. He knew it was ridiculous but he imagined her in his bed, running his hands over her smooth body.

He decided to phone Jessica and arrange to return her clothes and ask her to his boathouse next weekend.

He was on the steps of the National Maritime Museum when his phone rang. It was Morwenna. 'Giles, darling, how are you? You didn't deserve that awful intrusion last night. Quite unforgivable. I said to your father; "We must invite Giles down here next weekend to make up for it." I simply won't take no for an answer, darling; you can't keep hiding yourself away. You ought to get out more, you know.'

'Yes, mother.'

'Now, don't give it another thought. We're having some friends round; you remember Ted and Marion Lazenby don't you? Of course you do; just a little get-together, nothing fancy.'

Morwenna never did anything by halves. A little get-together would mean a full-blown dinner party and a weekend of golf, fishing or clay pigeon at the country club. Damn, that was next weekend with Jessica wiped out. On the other hand, he did need to speak to his father about divorcing Lydia.

'We'll see you on Friday night, then, about seven. Bye, darling.'

*

Jess was enjoying a lazy Sunday morning with Mandy's family. Trevor had the day off, something he made the most of when it came, and had cooked a Jamaican brunch of ripe banana fritters, avocado toast with fried eggs and hot and spicy sweet potatoes. Jess's taste buds were buzzing.

'Mm, this is scrummy, Trevor. Where d'you learn to cook like that?'

He replied in his laid-back way. 'Oh, ma mother, she always encourage me to cook at home.'

'Where was home?'

'Pimlico. Ma dad was friends with Frank Bruno when they was growin' up.'

'Oh, cool. Did your dad box, too?'

Trevor shook his head. 'Nah, but Frank made it big and we was happy for him.'

Mandy gave her husband a sideways look. 'Heard it all before, love.'

'Jess hasn't.'

Jess smiled. 'Do your parents still live there?'

Trevor shook his head. 'They live not far from here. Dad wanted to go back to Jamaica but Mum wouldn't.' He looked at Mandy, 'We'll pop round later, yeah?'

Mandy nodded and took the dishes out to the kitchen.

Jess followed. 'Here, I'll help you clear up.'

'No need. I'm fine,' said Mandy, taking the dirty plates to the dishwasher. 'So, what *are* you gonna do about Giles?' asked Mandy.

'I dunno. I've still got to pick me clothes up from his place at some point.'

'Maybe he'll post 'em to you!'

'I wouldn't put it past him. Either that or get Benson to bring 'em round here.'

'Benson?'

'His chauffer.'

'Gawd. What's the story there, then?'

Jess shrugged, 'He didn't talk the whole way to Greenwich. I reckon he lives on his own, though. Seems like he's always on call so he must be tee-total.'

'Boring. Still, if it brings in the dosh...'

Trevor poked his head round the door. 'I'm takin' the girls up the park, OK?'

'Yeah, fine. See you later.' Mandy turned to Jess. 'What d'you wanna do now then?'

'I suppose I ought to go. I need to get some shopping before they close.' Jess looked down at her dress and silver sandals from last night. 'I feel a bit overdressed in this lot, though!'

'You could borrow a pair of me jeans and a top?'

'Nah, it's OK. You've done enough. I'll nip home first.'

'I don't mind, it's been nice having you here.'

'Yeah, thanks Mandy.'

Mandy saw Jess to the door. 'I'll have an hour of Me Time while they're out. See you tomorrow.'

*

Jess had just come in when her phone bleeped. She quickly dropped her shopping in the kitchen and answered it.

'Jessica. It's Giles.'

'Oh, hi.'

'I er ...you left your clothes here last night. I was wondering...'

'...that's OK. I'll come and pick 'em up, maybe one evening?'

'Well, no...actually... I need to make amends for that fiasco last night. If you're not waiting for them, I was going to ask you to my boathouse the weekend after next. I could return them to you then.'

'OK, cool.'

'I'll get Benson to come for you on the Friday evening, then?'

'Yeah, I'll have to ask for time off, though. Is it OK if I let you know in the week?'

'Of course. I look forward to hearing from you.'

*

Jess arrived at Jenkins & Co. dead on 9 o'clock on Tuesday morning immaculately dressed in a light blue skirt suit and crisp white blouse. Chris glowed as he greeted her and introduced her to Cynthia and Janet both dressed in twin sets and pearls like two old aunts. Cynthia poured her a cup of coffee while Chris went through the things that would be expected of her, explaining that he had two other offices and he flitted about between them as necessary. He was hoping to take life a bit easier now and asked Jess, when she became confident, if she wouldn't mind him offloading some of the work onto her. She welcomed it. *Much better than pandering to Liz's silver surfers.*

Chris had two valuation appointments today with clients hoping to put their properties on the market. While Chris drove, he told Jess what she could expect whilst out on the road with him. 'First and foremost I expect my staff to put my clients at ease and listen very carefully to their requirements. We need to be seen as professional and attentive. Wouldn't you agree?'

'Oh, yeah, very much so.'

He glanced at her. 'I think you'll be fine.'

The first property was a very bog-standard two-up two-down terraced house on a 1970s estate. Mrs Brown answered the door with one snotty-nosed child on her hip and another clinging to her skirt. Jess noticed she had another on the way and was reminded of some of the women on the scruffy estate where she grew up.

Through the narrow, dark and depressing hall, the walls painted a dark blue, Jess and Chris followed Mrs Brown into the living room. Mr Brown stepped forward and gave his wife a reprimanding look, hastily brushed some crumbs off the sofa and cleared away some toys to make room for Chris and Jess to sit down. They found it difficult to talk to the couple with both children whining, so Jess encouraged the older child, a little boy, to come to her and show her one of his toys. Mrs Brown looked relieved but Jess hadn't banked on the sticky fingers he was now wiping down her pristine blue skirt. Jess tried to ignore it and remain focused, all the time listening to the conversation. But when she went upstairs with Chris to measure the dimensions of the rooms, she quickly went to the bathroom and tried to find a clean face cloth with which to sponge down her skirt. She was out of luck. She had to make do with a corner of a towel that looked as though it could do with a boil wash and hoped for the best. Chris was oblivious to her plight and came to ask her what she thought would help to sell the property.

'Well, I'd get rid of all the clutter for a start.' A steam-clean wouldn't go amiss, either, thought Jess but she kept that to herself. 'Houses that are clean and tidy create the illusion of space, makes 'em easier to sell.'

Chris lifted his eyebrows. 'Absolutely. Anything else?'

'Yeah, I'd advise 'em to replace the dark walls with a light colour, make it look bigger.'

'You could – it depends if they're willing. You need to be tactful and get all this across to Mr and Mrs Brown. You OK with that?'

Jess nodded. She'd bitten her tongue so many times in the salon it was a wonder it was still intact.

'Excellent. I knew I'd made the right decision when I asked you to join me.'

They went downstairs to assess the ground floor rooms. There wasn't a square foot without clutter of some kind but they did their best without bumping into each other. At the kitchen door Jess caught a glimpse of the overflowing rubbish bin and the washing-up stacked at the sink and she felt sorry for Mrs Brown whose husband was obviously averse to rolling his sleeves up and getting stuck in.

Jess returned to the living room and told Mr Brown what they suggested but he was on the defensive. 'But I like the rich brown walls in here; I chose that colour myself. It's cosy. Is it really necessary to paint them a cold cream?'

Chris looked at Jess and waited for her to explain.

'Well, it's up to you but light colours are in vogue, Mr Brown,' she began, 'They give the illusion of space and light, always a plus when selling a house.'

Mrs Brown's eyebrows shot up as if to say, I told you so. Her husband realised he was outnumbered. 'Oh all right, if that's what it takes. I don't wholly agree but we are looking for a quick sale,' he said, looking at his wife's advanced state of pregnancy. 'We desperately need more space.'

Chris came up with a 'realistic' figure and told them to get in touch when they had completed the necessary work and he would send round a photographer.

Satisfied they had done all they could, Chris took Jess to a little back street café to discuss their morning over a bite of lunch. She noticed the café needed some serious updating but when she told Chris, he defended it saying it was a handy place to eat whilst out on the road.

'Oh, don't get me wrong,' said Jess, 'it's just ... I notice things.'

He stroked his beard thoughtfully and scanned the décor.

They ordered sandwiches and mugs of tea at the counter, Jess all the while noticing how things were done. If she owned this café she would certainly knock it into shape. She'd get rid of the sloppy assistant with greasy hair for a start. Their sandwiches and drinks were begrudgingly set on the tray in front of them and Chris handed over the money.

Taking the tray to the only cleared table, Chris sat down and put on his serious face. 'The way things are at the moment, selling property has never been such a challenge. The market is in a constant state of flux. Since the credit crunch the average price of property has plummeted, then risen then fallen again.' He noticed how she dropped her eyes. 'Sorry to sound off-putting, but we have to be vigilant in the property business if we're to survive. There's a lot of competition out there, Jess.'

Jess nodded. 'Of course.'

The assistant wiped over the neighbouring table with a tea-stained cloth.

Chris saw Jess's reaction. 'Yes, I know. I'll have to find another cafe!'

The next property was a four bedroom detached house in a residential area. It would have been a sought-after property in its day but it now looked a bit sad and neglected. Mr Holsworthy was an elderly man who wanted to move to a sheltered flat. He proudly showed them around and told them he'd lived in the same house with his late wife for a good many years; so long in fact, that he'd forgotten what made him buy the house in the first place.

'My dear wife loved it here, always maintained that the only way she'd leave was in a wooden box, which indeed she did, bless her.'

Chris turned away and began writing on his notepad as he wandered into the next room. Jess thought that was a bit off and asked Mr Holsworthy, 'Did your wife have many friends?'

'Oh, yes. She was very popular, always going to ladies clubs and the like. She was a lovely person. I miss her greatly.'

'I'm sorry,' she wanted to learn more but looked in the direction of the stairs. 'I think I'm needed up there.'

'Of course, my dear. I'll make some tea for when you come down.'

Chris was in and out of the bedrooms taking notes. He looked up when he heard Jess. 'Everything all right?'

She nodded and went to look at the bathroom. A pink suite and frilly curtains – it obviously hadn't been touched for years. There were some grab rails on the wall by the toilet and near the bath and Jess had an image of Mr Holsworthy helping his wife to stand up. The lump in her throat took her by surprise.

Chris finished his note-taking and came to find her. 'OK Jess. I think that's it up here. What do you think?'

'About what?' she came to her senses, 'Oh sorry, I was just thinking about poor Mr Holsworthy and what it must've been like before his wife died.'

'You can't afford to get too emotional in this job, Jess. It's the properties we're assessing, not the occupants.'

'I know but...'

Chris didn't wait to hear any more. He went downstairs and Jess followed.

While Mr Holsworthy was in the kitchen, Chris asked Jess what she thought would help to sell the property.

'Maybe the kitchen needs replacing but it's not worth him doing that – the new owners would only rip it out and put their own in, but the floor could do with some new vinyl. Apart from that, I think the house is in good nick, sorry, condition, just a bit outdated. He could de-clutter and maybe take the old net curtains down to let in more light. The bathroom needs attention but nothing that a good spring clean wouldn't sort out. A man living on his own...well, you know.'

Chris looked sideways at her as if he knew what she was thinking about him but he nodded in agreement, all the time taking notes.

Mr Holsworthy staggered back in with a tray of jingling cups and saucers. Jess ran to his rescue before he dropped the lot on the floor and set them on the coffee table. She noticed he'd opened a packet of chocolate digestives. Ah, bless – he probably never had visitors. The tea was lukewarm but she didn't want to disappoint him so she drank it in one gulp. Mr Holsworthy looked pleased. 'Another cup?'

She shook her head. 'That was just enough, thank you.'

Chris left his and said, 'We'll just take a look outside now, if that's all right?'

Mr Holsworthy nodded. 'I won't come out. You'll be all right without me, won't you?'

'Of course.'

Outside, Chris and Jess surveyed the back garden and Jess noticed a couple of steps were broken. 'Should he replace those?'

'Not really necessary. As long the garden is tidy the prospective buyers won't put that at the top of their list.'

Chris looked very pleased with the way Jess spoke to their client.

Back at the office, Chris went through a few formalities and asked Jess when she could start.

'I'll have to hand me notice in and let you know. Is that all right?'

'Absolutely. I look forward to hearing from you, Jess.' They shook hands.

Yes! She'd clinched it. She was looking forward to working for Jenkins & Co and couldn't wait to see Liz's face when she told her to stuff her job.

*

The next day, Mandy was chatting to Connie in the staffroom when Jess burst in. She was just about to tell Mandy about her day with Chris Jenkins when Liz came storming through the salon and opened the staffroom door.

'Where the hell have you been? I've got a shop full of clients and I've nearly finished Mrs Robinson. Get the coffee on and hurry up!'

Jess sauntered into the salon and up to the desk. After yesterday, she wasn't bothered – Liz could do what she liked.

Now for the question, 'By the way, Saturday after next, can I have the day off?'

'You've got a nerve!'

Mrs Robinson put in her two penn'worth, 'Really, Jess. It's not good enough, you know…'

'Mind your own business, you nosey old cow!'

'Well, really!'

Jess was elated. She'd wanted to shut her up for years.

'That's enough!' said Liz, 'get your things and go. You're fired!'

'Don't worry. I'm going…. I've got another job, anyway.'

Liz glared at her. 'Huh, who'd want to employ you?'

'You'd be surprised.' Jess stuck her nose in the air and walked smartly back to the staff room. A blanket of silence fell on the salon, the only sound coming from the water spray where Paris was shampooing.

In the staffroom, Jess grabbed her handbag and said to Mandy, 'That's it, I'm done. I'll phone you later.'

'Good luck!'

'Thanks.'

A little while later, Eddie stuck his head round the back door of Top to Toe. 'Hi, Mandy. Is Jess about?'

'She's gone home, Eddie. Liz has fired her.'

'What? I was gonna MOT her car this morning. OK, I'll pop round and see her.'

When Eddie went round to Jess's flat, he expected to find her in tears but she surprised him – she was humming along to the radio, making a cup of tea.

'What's going on? Mandy told me you got the bullet.'

'Yeah,' she grinned, 'but I've got a better job.'

'Oh? When did this happen?'

'Yesterday, Jenkins estate agents. Cool, eh?'

Eddie frowned. 'Estate agents? But you don't know the first thing about that.'

'Don't I?' She beamed.

Jess was so excited she couldn't stop talking about it. Although Eddie was pleased for her he wasn't really listening. When he asked for her car keys it was clear to him that she'd forgotten all about the MOT and probably, he thought sadly, about him too.

When Eddie had driven her car away, Jess rang Mandy who had nipped out to buy a sandwich. Jess told her all about her morning with Chris Jenkins.

'Sounds great but he hasn't tried anything, has he?'

'Don't worry; I don't think he's got it in him!'

'Ha! So when do you start?'

'I'm not sure. I tried to ring him earlier but I got his voicemail. I left a message saying I can start anytime.' She looked at her watch. 'Actually, I'd better get off this phone. He might be trying to ring me.'

She was right. Chris rang as soon as she'd hung up. 'Jess, got your message. Can you meet me tomorrow – same time, same place?'

'Of course. Look forward to it.'

Eddie brought Jess's car back with the necessary paperwork. Everything was in order; her little bubblegum pink Ka had passed its MOT. He'd replaced the worn wiper blades but didn't tell her he'd paid for that. He handed her the keys. 'That's it. All done for another year.'

'Thanks, Eddie. I'm gonna need me car more than ever now. I'll be flitting about all over the place. It'll be great. Aren't you proud of me?'

Eddie wasn't sure; he didn't know her anymore.

'Want some lunch?'

'Nah… I'll pass thanks. Busy day.'

∗

Giles hadn't been able to get Jess out of his mind. He'd been walking about like a love-sick teenager since Saturday night, and this evening, he decided to go round to what he thought was her house, and surprise her.

A tall clean shaven black man came to the door. Giles looked askance and asked if Jessica was there but the man turned and shouted into the hall, 'There's somebody asking for Jess, love.'

A woman with multi-coloured hair appeared wiping her hands on a towel, followed by two little girls. 'Sorry, she's not here. Can I give her a message?'

'Yes, er... if you could tell her Giles Morgan called? Thanks,' he smiled briefly and turned back to his Mercedes.

Mandy slammed the door and turned to Trevor, 'Oh my God. I'd better ring Jess and warn her.'

Trevor was also in the dark. 'What? Who was that? And what did he want?'

'Tell you later.' Mandy picked up her mobile.

Jess answered straight away. 'Oh my God. You didn't tell him where I lived?'

'No, course not, but he looked a bit put out.'

'Phew! So what did you tell him?'

'I just said you weren't here.'

'OK. Thanks, Mandy. I'll phone him later.'

'Sooner you than me, explaining that one.'

Exactly. What the hell was she going to tell Giles? She hadn't really thought this through. Jess went to the fridge and poured herself a glass of wine and went over the possibilities.
Number one: she could say that Mandy was her sister who had come to stay for a few days with her husband and twins.
Number two: she could tell Giles that she was staying with her sister for a while and that she had just popped out for a carton of milk, that's why he'd missed her.
Or Number three: she could come clean with him.

Jess decided on number two. She'd say she was staying with Mandy for a few weeks. But wait – what would be the reason? No. If she wasn't careful she'd be digging herself into an even deeper hole. That wouldn't work. On second thoughts it would have to be number one. She would tell Giles that Mandy had come to stay for a couple of days. She certainly couldn't tell him the truth. Not yet.

Jess took a deep breath and rang Giles.

'Giles Morgan.'

'Oh, hi. It's me, Jessica.'

He felt nineteen again. 'Jessica! I tried to see you this evening.'

'Yeah, I know...sorry about that. That was my sister you spoke to....she's come to stay for a couple of days.'

'I see. I wanted to ask you how you got on yesterday.'

'Yesterday? Oh, great, thanks. I got the job.'

'But... I thought you had an appointment with an estate agent?'

'Yeah, I did.'

'I'm sorry?'

Jess knew he wanted an explanation. 'Look, I didn't tell you I was going after the job in case I didn't get it.OK?'

'Right. So who will you be working for?' Giles thought he ought to show some interest.

'Jenkins & Co. I'll be sales negotiator. Cool, eh?'

'If you say so.'

Jess was disappointed, she thought Giles would be only too pleased for her. 'Ooh, by the way. I've got Saturdays off now.'

'Wonderful. I'll get Benson to pick you up a week on Friday.'

CHAPTER EIGHT

Giles drove up outside Twin Oaks, his parents' grade II listed Georgian residence in Kent. The house took its name from the two huge oak trees that stood one each side of the wrought iron gates which automatically swung open allowing him to drive in. As he approached the house he spotted an Audi parked in front of the west wing. Dammit, he'd hoped to grab a couple of hours with his father to discuss the Lydia problem before the others arrived but this looked less than likely now.

As he entered the large porch his mother rushed out looking immaculate as ever and greeted him with open arms, her bracelets jangling. 'Giles, darling. You're looking tired.' She reached up to kiss his cheek and pushed a strand of hair back from his forehead. 'Come into the lounge, Ted and Marion have just arrived; had a pretty awful journey by all accounts.'

Giles breathed in the familiar smell of her and wished he could enjoy the evening with his parents alone, instead of putting on a front for two people he didn't care for. He wanted to relax. Jasper, their black Labrador, came bounding up to him, putting a smile on his face.

'Hello, boy.' He roughed up the dog's fur.

Giles followed his mother through the high-ceilinged hall towards the lounge. Jasper followed on behind, wagging his tail. The other couple were perched on the edge of one of the big white sofas with drinks, looking pensive.

Morwenna rushed forward in a flurry of excitement. 'You remember Ted and Marion, don't you, Giles?'

'Yes, of course.' He forced a smile and shook hands with Ted who immediately stood to attention. He then bent down to kiss Marion on the cheek. He wasn't in the mood for small talk but thought he ought to comply for his mother's sake. 'I hear you had a bad journey?'

'Bloody awful, if you must know,' said Ted. 'The roads get worse every day, especially that M20, bloody road works for miles. Nice to see you again, though. How's it going?'

How's what going? He couldn't stand all this idle chit-chat, never could. What was the point? 'Fine, thanks.'

Jacob had heard Giles's car pull up and strode into the room. 'Giles, how are you? You're looking tired. Let me get you a drink. The usual?'

Giles nodded, sat in an armchair and continued making a fuss of the dog. How was he going to get round to the subject of Lydia and the divorce? He really needed to take his father to one side.

Jacob went over to the antique console table, poured his son a single malt and handed it to him. 'Ted has an exhibition at The Turner Contemporary. Very prestigious, has he told you?'

Giles groaned inwardly. 'Is that right?'

'Yes. I consider myself very fortunate, very fortunate indeed,' said Ted with a smug grin. 'The curator invited me to exhibit some of my work after seeing an exhibition of mine in our local village hall.'

'Really?' From what Giles had seen of Ted's work he couldn't understand what all the fuss was about – a chimpanzee could do it. 'I'm not a fan of modern art myself.'

Morwenna flushed scarlet. 'Giles isn't feeling very well tonight, are you darling?'

'I'm fine mother.'

They all looked awkwardly at each other until Marion chipped in. 'I think this new collection is very different from anything Ted's done before. It seems to be making waves in the art world. Isn't that right, dear?'

Ted gave a snort, 'Yes, especially as the title is Sea Pictures!'

Some forced laughter ensued.

'Excuse me,' said Giles and got up to fetch his holdall from the car. If he stayed in the room any longer he would probably throw up.

Morwenna felt she needed to explain and told her guests that Giles was very stressed at the moment; Lydia was up to her old tricks again.

'Oh, dear. That must be very difficult,' said Marion.

'Yes… well, we spoke to her yesterday and she seems eager to make amends. In fact, we've invited her over tomorrow evening…' Morwenna looked nervously in the direction that Giles had just walked, and Jacob, who gave her a flashing smile of reassurance.

Marion was doubtful 'Oh, dear. I hope we won't be in the way?'

'Not at all,' said Jacob, 'Lydia loves a good dinner party. She can be very entertaining, you know.'

'Absolutely,' said Ted who was looking forward to seeing Lydia again. 'I'm sure it'll be fine.'

Jacob decided a little light music would diffuse the atmosphere and moved over to the shiny grand piano and started to play one of his own compositions.

Feeling like a spare part, Ted took his drink over to the Georgian window in the alcove to focus on the pretty garden while Morwenna sat down beside Marion and took her into her confidence. 'I'm afraid it was all rather ghastly last Saturday evening.'

'Why? What happened?'

Morwenna took a deep breath. 'Well, it was Giles's fortieth, as you know, but unbeknown to us, he'd invited another girl along to the yacht club. Lydia, we thought, was in the south of France, but she burst in and made a terrible scene.'

'Oh, dear.'

'Yes, quite.' Morwenna studied her long tapered fingers and twisted one of her rings. 'Giles and Lydia haven't been getting on too well of late but it's about time they ironed out their differences; they could be so good together.'

On hearing this, Ted returned from the alcove and exchanged glances with his wife that implied they doubted it.

Giles stuck his head round the door to see if he could grab a few minutes alone with his father but Jacob was so engrossed in his piano that he gave it up as a bad job. He decided to have a walk in the garden instead.

Back in the lounge Morwenna announced that the buffet was now served in the dining room, courtesy of Fortnum and Mason. As she led the way she gave a nervous little laugh. 'Don't worry, I've asked the caterers to come in tomorrow evening. I'm afraid the days of the resident cook-cum-housekeeper have long gone, more's the pity. Perhaps you'd like to see the new conservatory later?'

Giles joined them just as Jacob was explaining the itinerary for the next day: a spot of golf and clay pigeon shooting at The Warren.

Just as he'd thought. Giles had lost his appetite. If only it were just him and his father on the golf course – it had been ages since the two of them had spent any time together.

Morwenna picked up the vibe from Giles and tried to smooth his ruffled feathers. 'I'm sure you'll enjoy it, darling. When did you last spend some time at The Warren? Some fresh air will do you good.'

CHAPTER NINE

Jess couldn't remember the last time she'd had a Saturday off. She decided to celebrate and take herself off for some retail therapy. Testing some new eye shadows at the cosmetic counter in Debenhams, she looked up and spotted a girl with short, spiky red hair. 'Becks! Becky?'

The girl looked round. 'Oh my God, Jess! It's been ages. How are you?'

'Not bad. I've got a new job!'

'Me too. Got loads to tell you. Fancy a coffee?'

'Cool.'

They sat upstairs in the restaurant with their cappuccinos and caught up with each other's news. Becky told Jess she now had her own mobile catering business called Dinner Parties4U.Com., cooking gourmet meals for people in their own homes. 'It's really fun, Jess, and I get to cook in some fab places. Money's not bad either. Take tonight: I've got six to cook for in a posh place near Maidstone. What you doing tonight?'

'Nothing much. But next Saturday I'll be with my hot-and-loaded boyfriend in his boathouse on the south coast.'

'Oh, yeah? Mine's busy tonight, too,' Becky laughed at her own joke.

'No, seriously. He's a lawyer. You should see his apartment at Greenwich!'

'Wow!'

'Yeah, I know, right.'

Becky wasn't really listening as Jess told her how she'd met Giles. She drank her coffee and sank into her own thoughts until, 'You up for helping me tonight, then? Kaz has cried off with a bad cold. You like cooking, don't you?'

'Yeah why not? Sounds like fun.'

'Cool. Come to mine about four o' clock?'

'Do I need to bring anything?'

'Nope, just your lovely self!'

Becky's remark gave Jess a warm glow. She was looking forward to her evening with her old friend who used to work at Top to Toe, and as Becky said, she got to cook in some fab places.

*

Just as Giles had predicted, Ted made a complete arse of himself at The Warren. Prior to the clay pigeon shoot, he was bragging about his prowess but he looked pretty silly when he started shooting into mid-air missing the targets. He complained, saying things like he wasn't used to plastic clays, he was a bit rusty and it was all a long time ago. The more Ted tried to dig himself out the worse it got. It was the same with the golf in the afternoon. It was quite obvious Ted had never lifted a golf club but still kept up the pretence that he knew exactly what he was doing. It was embarrassing for poor Marion but she wriggled out of the situation and went for a swim in the indoor pool with Morwenna. As for Giles, he always felt better in the fresh air. He ignored Ted's remarks and began to relax into the game with his father.

As they approached Twin Oaks at five thirty, Giles noticed a bright pink Ford Ka parked on the drive. His stomach flipped. There was only one person he knew with a car that colour.

The Range Rover spewed out its passengers noisily onto the gravel and they all headed for the house, except for Jacob, who drove the vehicle round to the coach house to put it away.

Giles turned to his mother. 'Whose car is that?'

'I should think it's the caterers, darling. Why?'

'Oh. Nothing.' The caterers? But Jessica said her new job was in estate agency. This was all very odd.

'Dinner's at eight, everyone,' shouted Morwenna, as she entered the hall, Jasper at her heels. 'Meet for drinks in the lounge at seven.'

*

Becky had been standing on her front step, looking at her watch, when Jess arrived. Jess shouted from the car window, 'Wassup? Not late, am I?'

'I can't get me car started, Jess. I don't know what's wrong with it. Can we use yours?'

'Sure.'

They loaded all the covered containers and cool boxes into Jess's little Ka and set off a little later than Becky would've liked. When they arrived at Twin Oaks, Jess drove up in front of the wrought iron gates and Becky shot out, punched in a code on the gate post and got back in the car. The gates swung open.

'Awesome,' said Jess. 'They trust you with the code, then?'

'Yeah, but I think they change it quite often. The family have electronic tags on their cars so the gates open automatically when they drive up.'

Jess was still taking this in when she parked on the gravel drive. Becky jumped out and punched in another number for the back door and they started to unload their equipment. Jess stood in awe of the huge kitchen fitted with grey-green units and an island in the middle. On the wall above the range cooker hung a stack of shiny copper saucepans.

'Come on, no time to stand gawping.' Becky took a bottle of white wine from one of the cool boxes and poured two glasses, turned the dial on her iPod dock to 'Ed Sheeran' and they started to prepare the first course – smoked salmon pâté.

Becky was all ears listening to Jess's account of her first date with her 'loaded boyfriend' and the kitchen was buzzing with noise and laughter. The two girls worked happily together until Becky said she was going along to the dining room to check on a few things. Jess was happy to be immersed in her work and took the opportunity to examine everything including the real granite worktops and custom made units and tried to imagine what it would be like to live in a place like this.

In complete contrast, the mood in the lounge was funereal. Morwenna was on edge wondering how Lydia would behave. Giles was taking his time in making his appearance this evening and this put Ted and Marion on edge. But Morwenna thought it fell to her to try and pull her son and his wife back together. Jacob had agreed. They were still very friendly with Lydia's parents and if it came to the crunch it would do nothing for their relationship, not to mention the cost of the settlement. There could be serious repercussions.

Satisfied that everything was under control in the dining room, Becky came back and asked Jess to go and have a look before the guests took their seats.

On opening the panelled door Jess stood open-mouthed. The large polished antique table was laid with finest white linen napkins, crystal goblets and silver and in the centre stood a large arrangement of fresh flowers in pastel colours. Above the table hung a huge crystal chandelier and when Jess turned it on everything sparkled. Running her fingers over the smooth wood and padded blue velvet of the chairs, she wandered over to the French windows and saw two antique urns filled with purple pansies standing on the patio. Steps led up to a well manicured lawn beyond which was an arch full of pink climbing roses just coming into bloom. Through the arch Jess could see tall trees and a glimpse of a pastel green summer house to the far wall. Immediately to her right, through the window of the Victorian-style conservatory was a mixture of palms and exotic plants. She had only seen things like this in glossy magazines and couldn't imagine being surrounded by such luxury.

Jess's heart skipped a beat – someone was coming! She hid behind the door just in time before it swung open.

'Oh my God, Becks! I nearly had a heart attack. I thought you were one of them.'

'Nah, silly. You comin'?'

Jess took one last glance at the room and committed it to memory, quickly turned off the light and followed Becky back to the kitchen.

Upstairs, Giles was pacing the bedroom floor like an expectant father. If he'd known Lydia had been invited he would definitely have taken Jessica to the Solent this weekend. His mother had wanted to surprise him but Ted had let it slip when they came back this afternoon. But what was his mother thinking? And as for talking to his father about a divorce, forget it.

At seven fifteen, Lydia drove up in her red Mercedes convertible. Morwenna was out of the house like a shot. Jasper followed with an expression that said, 'oh, it's you', and slumped in a corner of the hallway.

'Lydia, darling. Lovely to see you. Good journey?'

'Not bad, Wenn. You're looking well. Whose is that ghastly little car on the drive?'

Morwenna glanced out. 'Oh, that. Belongs to caterers.'

'Thank God. I thought it was someone we knew!' She handed her mother-in-law an over-the-top bouquet in orange and russet and gave her a peck on the cheek. As Lydia flounced through the porch, Morwenna couldn't help but notice the black and red tight-fitting bodice that pushed her daughter-in-law's ample breasts up to boiling point and hoped it would have the desired effect on Giles.

When Lydia entered the lounge Giles had a similar expression on his face to Jasper. He was feeling very edgy especially with the pink car on the drive but he put on a show of affection for all concerned and greeted his wife with quick peck on the cheek. She looked frostily at him and turned away with a smirk. The atmosphere was as heavy as lead. Ted and Marion exchanged anxious glances.

Jacob was the only one who looked relaxed. He greeted Lydia with a kiss on her lips and a pat on her bottom. 'Lydia, you're looking splendid. I'll get you a drink then I thought we could bash out a duet, if you're game?'

'Great! I can't remember the last time I played on a grand.'

'You know Ted and Marion don't you?'

Lydia turned to see the couple perched on the sofa. 'Oh, yes. How are you both?'

'All the better for seeing you,' said Ted, with a wink.

Lydia averted her eyes, flirting with him. 'Flattery will get you everywhere, Teddy!'

Marion had a fixed grin in place trying not to let it slip.

Giles couldn't believe it. What was the matter with them all, for God's sake? It was quite sickening and he had the whole evening to get through.

'There's some champagne on ice, if someone can open it?' said Morwenna.

'Here, let me,' said Ted, who jumped up and took the bottle out of the ice bucket. 'What's the occasion?'

They all looked at one another. Morwenna came to the rescue. 'It was Giles's fortieth last weekend but we didn't really get round to celebrating it properly,' she laughed nervously.

This statement went completely over Ted's head while he struggled to open the bottle. Finally the cork flew up to the ceiling and the champagne spurted out in all directions. 'Oh! Ha, ha, just the job.' He handed the first flute to Giles and licked his fingers. 'Champers?'

'No, thanks, can't stand the stuff.' God, how much more of this twit would he have to stomach?

'I'll have yours!' said Lydia, grabbing the glass. 'Come on, Jacob. To the grand!' They sat down together and started to play *The Entertainer*. Ted handed glasses of the champagne to his hosts and then to his wife who began to unwind a little, tapping her feet to the music. Ted sat with a sickly grin on his face and Morwenna busied herself getting Giles another drink while he sat making a fuss of Jasper. It was as normal as it could be under the circumstances.

After a while Giles turned to his mother. 'How's Grandfather?'

'He's very well. We see him most weekends. He loves his new apartment at The Birches and I'm sure he'd appreciate a visit from you, darling.'

'Yes. I might drop in on him tomorrow.'

Lydia's ears pricked up. 'You could take me. I haven't seen old Sam for ages.'

Morwenna saw her opportunity. 'What a good idea! I'm sure he'd love to see you both. Together.'

'Yes, Giles,' Lydia stopped playing and sauntered over to her husband, sat on the arm of his chair and started to ruffle his hair. He jerked away. 'Don't.'

'Oh, come on, you old party pooper. Let your hair down for once.'

As if by magic, a smoke alarm went off somewhere in the vicinity of the kitchen. Morwenna was instantly on her feet but Giles saw his opportunity. 'Don't worry, I'll go.'

He could hear loud pop music and giggling as he walked towards the kitchen. As he opened the door to the passage, he saw Jessica standing on a chair fanning the smoke alarm with a tea towel to stop the noise. The sight of her made his heart leap.

She started when she saw him and nearly fell.

He rushed forward and caught the chair. 'Whoa! What are you doing here?'

'I'm helping Becks. Look. Come in here, I've got to rescue me toast.'

He followed her into the kitchen and saw the hive of activity. Becky looked a bit put out at seeing him in the kitchen but Jess treated it as the norm and introduced her to Giles.

'Awesome. So you two know each other?' asked Becky.

They both nodded.

Becky looked from one to the other. 'Right.'

Giles looked around the room, 'Is everything under control?'

Jess and Becky grinned at each other. 'Yep,' said Jess, 'Just a bit of a hiccup!' Becky and Jess both burst into giggles.

He wanted to ask Jessica how she came to be here but he realised that now wasn't a good time. 'OK, I can see you're busy. I'll leave you to it.'

So, it *was* Jessica's car on the drive. He only hoped Jessica would keep a low profile – he didn't want another scrap.

Back in the lounge, everyone stopped talking and looked up when Giles entered.

'Everything OK?' asked Morwenna.

Giles nodded, 'All under control.'

'Oh, good,' said Marion, 'I'm always a bit twitchy when I hear those things go off. Well, you never know, do you?'

'No, quite,' said Giles, and took up his place in the armchair again. Jacob and Lydia were back on the piano. Luckily for Giles she hadn't noticed the change in his demeanour.

Before long, Becky came into the lounge and announced that the first course, smoked salmon pâté, was now being served in the dining room.

'Oh, good,' said Ted, 'I'm running on empty.'

In the dining room, Morwenna gave out the order of the seating arrangements. She and Jacob were to sit one at each end of the table. Lydia was put next to Ted, who thought it was his lucky day, and Giles sat next to Marion. They all took their places and Jacob told them about the wines he had chosen for the evening – a white 1989 Burgundy with the first course and a 1998 Australian Shiraz from New South Wales for the main. He poured the white wine for the ladies first then Ted, then Giles and finally himself.

Lydia chinked glasses with Ted and took a mouthful, 'Mm, lovely,' and pinched Ted's thigh under the table, making him jump and spill his wine.

Marion glared at him. 'What do you think you're doing?' Her eyes darted around the table. 'I'm so sorry. I can't take him anywhere.'

'No problem,' said Lydia, 'I'll go and fetch a cloth.' She smiled cheekily at Ted and left the room.

Becky and Jess were so engrossed in their work and their music that they didn't notice Lydia until she turned to leave the kitchen.

Jess whispered in Becky's ear, 'Oh my God, Becks! That was the bitch from hell!'

'Who?'

'Giles's wife! Look. Last weekend I went with him to the yacht club for his fortieth birthday bash. She turned up and made a right scene. How the hell was I to know he had a wife?'

'Bloody Nora. Poor you.'

'Yeah. I ran out to the loo, tried to get a signal on me phone but there was nothing, not even a bar, so I cadged a taxi home. Well...to Mandy's.'

'What? Why Mandy's?'

'I was staying there. Long story. I'll tell you later. Anyway...'

'OK, I can see your problem but it really needs two of us to serve, Jess.' Becky thought about this. 'What if you tie your hair up; she mightn't recognise you.'

'All right, but I'll blame you if she twigs!'

Lydia came back into the dining room and glared at Giles. 'Well, there's something very fishy going on here and it's not just the smoked salmon pâté.'

Her remark fell on deaf ears as everyone was engaged in conversation. Marion was telling her husband to be more careful while Morwenna tried to smooth things over. Giles had heard Lydia's remark but chose to ignore it. Instead he became engrossed in his favourite subject. 'Yes,' he said to Jacob, 'I need to do some work on Sea Witch – her hull needs attention. Next weekend, maybe. Depends on the weather, of course.'

'I think you enjoy sailing as much as I like golf. Good round today, wasn't it?'

Giles nodded. He took a mouthful of wine and glanced at Ted who was oblivious to their conversation, his attention fixed on Lydia. 'Pity about you-know-who, still, it was quite funny when he missed the ball and landed on his arse! At least we completed the course, and you had a hole-in-one.'

Jacob smiled. 'Yes, that's a rare occurrence. But you did very well to say you haven't played for ages.'

'Thanks.'

Becky came in and started to clear away the remains of the first course. Giles tried to look as relaxed as possible and hoped Jessica wouldn't put in an appearance.

Morwenna announced that the main course was casserole of wild game.

Lydia seized her opportunity, 'Ooh, I like a bit of *wild game*, don't you Teddy?' and winked at him.

Ted beamed. 'Oh, rather!'

Giles looked daggers at her. Good God. If this was her trying to make amends she wasn't trying very hard.

Marion had shut up like a clam. Morwenna and Jacob looked at each other from opposite ends of the table wishing the main course would hurry up.

Morwenna broke the silence and asked Lydia if she would like to help her on the WI cake stall on the village green tomorrow.

'Well,' she feigned coyness for Ted's benefit, 'I was thinking of going to see old Sam. Might perk him up a bit, if you know what I mean.'

Ted giggled. She certainly perked him up. What he wouldn't give for a night in the sack with *her*!

Marion gave her husband a look that could have frozen Africa.

In came the girls with the wild game casserole. As they served, Lydia kept an eye on Giles to see if he gave anything away where Jess was concerned, but he kept his attention on his father. Lydia watched as Jess kept her back to them and her eyes averted while she helped Becky serve, then made a quick exit. Jess hovered on the other side of the closed door to hear the reaction.

Becky explained that the accompaniments were braised fennel and duchess potatoes, two of her friend's specialities.

'This looks excellent, I must say,' said Jacob and raised his glass. 'Our compliments to the chefs!'

Everyone followed suit.

Becky beamed and took a bow. 'Thanks. Enjoy.'

Back in the kitchen Jess and Becky gave themselves a high five and another glass of wine.

'Any more of this Becks and I won't be able to drive home. Oh my God! What we gonna do?

'Don't worry, it's sorted. Morwenna'll let us stay in the old servants' wing.'

'Really? I would've brought me tooth brush if I'd known.'

'No probs,' said Becky, as she put the plates in the dishwasher. 'Morwenna keeps a stack of spares.'

'Oh. Do you know her well, then?'

'Nah, but I've been here before. They're a nice family, the Morgans; always appreciate your efforts.'

The penny dropped with a massive clang. 'Oh my God! Did you say Morgans?'

'Well, yeah. I thought you knew?'

Jess's stomach flipped. She had thought that maybe Giles was visiting friends or something. Still, whatever happened, she definitely couldn't drive home tonight. God! She'd have a lot to tell Mandy next time they met.

With the dinner party in full swing and a lull before the dessert, Becky took Jess upstairs to show her the old servants' quarters. They took the back stairs so as not to bump into anyone.

It was an amazing old house and Jess imagined it must've been run like *Downton Abbey* years ago. There were two attic bedrooms with oak beams, prettily decorated with pale floral curtains and metal bedsteads and white bedding. Jess relished the idea of staying the night except for one tiny problem. Cruella. But at least the servants' wing was cut off from the rest of the house. She hoped for the best.

They ran back downstairs to clear away the remains of the main course and prepare and serve the desserts, before they were missed.

'I'll go fetch the plates Jess, if you can start the desserts?'

'Cool.'

While Becky was gathering the dirty plates in the dining room, she announced that the choice of desserts consisted of Lemon Sorbet or Chocolate Tipsy Tart. Lydia said she'd plump for the Lemon Sorbet as she was watching her figure and Ted, who felt brave by this time, said he wouldn't mind watching it for her. Marion gave Ted a 'wait-till-I-get-you-home' look and said she would also like the Lemon Sorbet, her face as sour as the dessert.

While they were deciding who was having what, Giles excused himself and sneaked off to the kitchen. He found Jessica on her own, engrossed in her work with her back to him. She glanced round when he opened the door. 'Oh, hi.'

'I hope you're not driving home tonight,' he said, indicating the empty wine bottles on the side.

'Course not. I'm not that stupid. I know what I'm doing, OK?' she turned her back on him and continued putting the curls on the chocolate desserts. 'Did you come in here just to tell me that?'

Giles stood watching her. 'No, of course not. I wanted to see you.'

Jess continued working with her back to him.

'So, what *are* you doing?'

'I'm staying the night in the servants' wing, all right?'

He turned her towards him hoping for a kiss.

She shrugged him off. 'You'd better get back to your party,' she said, checking behind him to make sure Lydia hadn't followed him in.

'What's the matter?'

'Aren't you worried your wife will find you here, with me?'

'Oh, all right,' he huffed, wrenched the door open and stormed off.

Becks came back with the tray of plates. 'Blimey, I nearly dropped the lot. Grumpy sod pushed past me with no 'sorry' or anything.'

'Yeah, he's been in here telling me not to drive home.'

'Bloody cheek!'

'I know, right.'

Back in the dining room Lydia looked up when Giles entered.

So did Morwenna. 'Oh, there you are, Giles. Chocolate Tipsy Tart or Lemon Sorbet?'

He was deep in thought. How was he expected to sleep with his wife when Jessica was in the servants' wing?

'Giles?'

'What? Oh ...er... I'll have the chocolate thing.'

Lydia saw her opening, 'I think there's more than one tipsy tart here tonight, isn't there, Giles?' she said, fixing him with a stare.

'Talking about yourself again, Lydia?'

She flipped the remark on its head. 'Am I a tipsy tart, Teddy?'

'I think you're lovely,' drooled Ted. He couldn't remember a time when he'd enjoyed himself so much. What a woman!

Jacob had to smile to himself; there was never a dull moment where his daughter-in-law was concerned. He couldn't understand why his son wasn't happy with her; she was quite a girl. Such a pity they lived separate lives. They really needed to sort things out once and for all.

While everyone was tucking into their desserts, Morwenna told them she would be serving coffee and liqueurs, later, in the new conservatory.

Ted was still fawning over Lydia and hanging on her every word. Marion gave her husband a look that could kill at ten paces.

'I know someone who's going to bed early...'

'Oh, now there's an invitation, Teddy!' said Lydia.

Ted smiled, imagining what it would be like to snuggle up to Lydia's voluptuous body but his brain was so fuddled he couldn't come up with a witty retort.

Becky and Jess started clearing up the kitchen, helped themselves to another glass of wine and a few leftovers and congratulated themselves on the success of the evening. 'It's been a blast, Becks!'

'Told you, and it ain't over yet. We get to sleep in those fab bedrooms with the shiny en-suites.'

'Yay!'

Back in the conservatory, Marion refused to let Ted have a liqueur and pushed a black coffee in front of him.

Giles had had enough. He announced he was turning in.

Lydia feigned a yawn, 'I think I'll join you.'

Jacob and Morwenna exchanged knowing glances but Giles was less than happy. Dammit, that was all he needed – to share a bed with the woman who he thought had made a real spectacle of herself tonight. He had been hoping to settle down with his new copy of *Yachting World* for an hour – it might have helped dispel any thoughts he had of Jessica, but now he doubted it would've made much difference. She was really getting under his skin.

In the bedroom over-looking the garden, Lydia and Giles ignored one another as they got undressed until Lydia remarked, 'Well, I've had a lovely time tonight; I must have made Ted's day.'

Giles raised his eyes to the ceiling. He thought the whole business had been pathetic and was on the verge of telling her so when she slid between the sheets and gave him her 'come-to-bed' look. He blew out a sigh; if he went to the guest room it would only seal her suspicions so he resigned himself to making an effort, got into the king-size bed, turned out the light and kept to his side of the bed. Lydia moved closer and started to tickle him. He shrugged her off.

'Oh, come on, Giley, don't be an old spoil sport, you know you like it, really.'

He didn't and it was even worse now, knowing where Jessica was tonight and he hated her using her pet name for him. After a few more attempts Lydia gave up, turned over and snored.

In the old servants' quarters, Becky and Jess said goodnight and went to their separate bedrooms. Jess wondered what it would have been like to be a servant here in days gone by. Not a bad life, really, all things considered; at least you had good food and a roof over your head. Better than the workhouse anyway, where she reckoned some of her ancestors had ended up.

After making use of the en-suite facilities she sank into the crisp, fresh sheets and closed her eyes. Immediately, images of Giles flashed onto her eyelids. She couldn't believe she had stumbled upon the Morgans' dinner party – what an eye-opener! The more she thought about it the more she wondered what it would be like to be part of their family, swanning around in designer clothes, being accepted into their society...

But then there was Eddie. Her guilty conscience refused to let her sleep. She tossed and turned for a whole hour after which the effects of the wine were starting to wear off and sleep would not come. There was just too much to think about. The full moon was shining invitingly through a crack in the curtains and she finally gave up, dressed and went to find her way out to the garden, hoping some fresh air would help.

Jess tip-toed down the back stairs and into the kitchen and through the back porch where she found the door that led outside, quietly slid the bolt and found she was in the garden beneath the pergola. She stood for a moment taking in the scene; the beautiful but now colourless garden took on a new ethereal quality in the moonlight. Then she noticed the black Labrador walking towards her wagging his tail. He looked friendly enough so she started to stroke him.

Oh my God. Someone was coming! She hid behind the water butt.

'Hello boy. Can't you sleep either?' Giles ruffled the dog's ears and chucked him under the chin. Jess watched for a while but just as she turned to go back inside Giles spotted her. 'Jessica!' he hissed.

She came out from the shadows and whispered. 'What are you doing here?'

'I couldn't sleep. So it seems, neither could you,' he whispered back.

He took her hand. 'Come with me.'

After thinking about Eddie she wasn't sure. 'But this is wrong – what about your wife?'

'Don't worry, Lydia's dead to the world. This way.' He led her up the steps and into the summer house and closed the door quietly behind them.

They didn't hear or see Lydia who had come down to spy on Giles. She took out her mobile from her dressing gown pocket. Click! Just the evidence she needed.

CHAPTER TEN

Giles felt renewed. Jessica had been reluctant at first but in the end she had succumbed and was a willing bed partner and they had finally cancelled out at 4am. And now he crept back to the bedroom to take a shower in the en-suite, hoping he hadn't been missed. Lydia was still snoring in the same position in which he'd left her last night so he felt fairly confident.

Feeling ravenous he was the first down to breakfast. The early morning sun was streaming through the French doors into the dining room as he helped himself to a bowl of muesli and some fresh fruit from the breakfast buffet on the sideboard, his mind still on Jessica. Jasper wandered in wagging his tail, hoping for a tasty morsel and Giles hoped the dog was the only one that knew of his midnight liaison. He had surprised himself last night. He'd never done anything so rash, but he was apprehensive about any consequences that might follow and also what his grandfather would make of it all when he went to see him later. Giles finished his breakfast, found Jasper's lead hanging on the hall stand and took him out for a walk.

Morwenna and Jacob were next down to breakfast, followed by Lydia who rushed downstairs and stopped in the doorway. 'I'll pass on breakfast, if you don't mind, Wenn. I've got a few things to tie up before I go back to France. I'll see old Sam another time. Au revoir.' and off she went.

Jacob and Morwenna looked at each other. Last night obviously hadn't been the success they were hoping for.

Ted and Marion wandered in. Ted was looking decidedly green around the gills and said he'd skip breakfast.

'I know what you need,' said Jacob, and went to the kitchen.

'Serves him right,' said Marion and moved over to the smorgasbord of delights.

Jacob came back and handed Ted a raw egg concoction. 'Here, down the hatch.'

Giles sauntered back from his walk with Jasper, feeling rejuvenated but his mood changed when he saw the ominous dry patch Lydia's car had left behind. He went inside hoping at last to have that talk with his father but he was still out of luck – Ted and Marion were still hogging the limelight. Ted was sitting at the table holding his head and groaning.

'I hope you're not going to drive home in that state?' said Giles. 'You'll still be over the legal limit, you know?'

Marion was quick to jump in. 'Oh no, don't worry. I'm driving. I didn't have much to drink last night.'

'Good.' Giles moved towards the door, hoping to find Jessica before she left.

'You're not skipping breakfast, too, are you Giles?' asked his mother.

'I had mine earlier and took Jasper out for a walk.'

'Gosh! That fresh air must've done you good yesterday. I can't remember the last time you did that.'

Giles heard a car engine roar into life and turned to see the back of Jessica's pink KA as she drove through the gates. Dammit.

Later that morning Giles drove into the grounds of The Birches, a new complex of retirement apartments set within a copse of silver birch trees, where his grandfather resided. Giles locked his Mercedes and buzzed his grandfather on the side panel of the main door.

'Grandfather, it's me, Giles.'

'Giles! Come on up.'

On the first floor he tapped on his grandfather's door.

Samuel Morgan greeted him with a bright smile. 'What a lovely surprise. Do come in.' He had the appearance of a wise old owl, a sprightly man in his nineties with a head of thick, white hair. Giles followed his grandfather through to the large sitting room overlooking the manicured communal gardens and the rolling countryside beyond.

Sam went to the picture window. 'I've been watching the birds – the feathered variety, I hasten to add!' He picked up his binoculars from the sideboard. 'There was a lovely little wren out there a moment ago. Delightful little birds.'

When there was no response from Giles, Sam put down his binoculars and turned to him. 'I see you're on your own?'

Giles nodded.

'How is Lydia?'

Giles sat down and ran a hand over his face.

'Oh, dear. Like that is it?'

'We live separate lives now – she's mainly in France while I'm in London. It's been like that for ages.'

'Oh? You do surprise me. But then again, I'm afraid Lydia's what we used to call a 'good time girl.' Maybe you're not really suited?'

'No...'

There was a long pause. How to tell his grandfather that Lydia suspected him of having an affair? This much was obvious to Giles since she had left so abruptly this morning. He wasn't sure what Sam would make of Jessica either.

Finally he said, 'I've met someone but I don't know what you'll make of her; she's not exactly from our class.'

Sam said, 'I see.' He thought for a while. There was something Giles ought to know about his past but Sam thought it would probably come as a shock. Nevertheless, he should tell him. 'You know, when I married Fran, she wasn't from our class, as you put it, she came from the East End, but she was a good woman. The best. We were perfectly suited and I miss her dreadfully.'

Giles was struck dumb. He had no idea his favourite grandmother was from the working class; she was always immaculately dressed and her speech impeccable. As far back as he could remember they had been a devoted couple from the same background, or so he thought.

Sam thought he ought to explain. 'The war was a great leveller, Giles. People from all walks of life found themselves caught up in the same situation. Fran lost all her family in an air raid while she was on night shift nursing at the Whitechapel hospital; a dreadful thing to lose all your family like that.' He went on to tell Giles how he had met Fran. 'I was home on leave with a chap I'd met in France. He took me to his home in the East End. His family had come to Fran's aid when she was made homeless, took her in. I was smitten as soon as I saw her and we started courting. Ha, that's what we called it in those days.' He smiled at the memory. 'We got married in 1946. I don't know if you know this but she was my second wife; the first was a woman approved of by my parents. We were poles apart. I divorced her and married Fran. Best thing I ever did.

'I had a good life with Fran and when she died two years ago, I took a downward turn, as you know. It was as though a part of me had died with her. But now, thankfully, I'm on the mend. I've made some lovely new friends here and slowly, one day at a time, I'm coming to terms with her absence and life is treating me well.'

'I'm sorry. I had no idea. About Gran's background, I mean.'

'No. I suspected as much. You see Giles, money's not everything. Fran came from a very respectable family even though they were poor.'

Giles was beginning to make comparisons with Jessica and his grandmother. Perhaps it could all work out for him.

After Giles had talked non-stop about Jessica, Sam said, 'Well, my advice Giles, speaking from experience, would be to follow your heart and do what you think fit. You're not a teenager anymore and you're not answerable to anyone. Live your own life and bugger what everyone else thinks.'

Giles nodded. 'There's only one snag.'

'What's that?'

'I stand to lose a lot of money in the divorce settlement.'

'Ah. In that case, my boy, you'll have to decide what takes priority.'

*

After dropping Becks off, Jess was looking forward to relaxing with a nice cup of tea, but as she pulled up outside Victoria Villas she noticed the main door to the flats was open. As she approached on foot, she realised not only was the door open but there was broken glass on the floor. A cold shiver ran through her as she tentatively stepped over the debris. She found Rose standing in her own doorway, looking stunned. She stared at Jess as if she was a stranger.

'What's happened?' asked Jess. 'What's going on?'

'We've had a break-in... terrible mess.... the Old Bill's just left. They don't hold out much hope though.'

'Oh my God.' Jess looked up the stairs to her own flat. The door was ajar.

'I'm waiting for the carpenter to come and do something with the doors and the locks'll have to be changed.' Rose went on to explain that she too had been away last night, at her sister's, and it wouldn't have happened if Sandy had heard them – he was a good guard dog.

Jess took a deep breath and tiptoed nervously upstairs. Not knowing what she'd find her heartbeat quickened. She stood in the doorway and stared round in disbelief. The place was trashed – curtains pulled down, spray paint up the walls. Some of the drawers had been emptied onto the floor and there was a big gaping hole where her telly and DVD player had been. She pushed open her bedroom door and saw that her bed was dishevelled but luckily nothing else in there had been touched, as if the burglars had been interrupted. Jess felt sick. Tears pricked her eyes. Why her? She didn't have much to start with – this was so unfair. What was she going to do now?

There was only one thing to do. She rang Mandy.

'You've been what?'

Jess blew her nose and talked through her tears. 'I dunno know what to do. I can't stay here. It feels dirty. Oh, it's so horrible Mandy, not like mine anymore.'

'The bastards! Of course you can't, come to us. I'll see you in a little while. We'll get it sorted, don't worry.'

Jess couldn't leave the flat quick enough. She took her overnight bag and stuffed in some clean underwear and clothes and ran downstairs past Rose who was still looking dazed and drove as fast as the speed limit would allow.

Jess burst through Mandy's door.

'Aw, come here.' Mandy hugged her and rubbed her back like her Nan used to do when she was little. It made her burst into a fresh bout of sobs. 'Oh, Jess. Go and sit down and I'll make you a cuppa.'

Mandy set the kettle to boil and came back and sat next to Jess. 'What did they take?'

'All my telly and stuff. And the mess, you wouldn't believe it, that's the worst thing. Why did they have to spray paint up the walls?' She was still shaking. She blew her nose.

Mandy shook her head.

'Luckily, they didn't get me bit of jewellery or me money – I had it all with me. I've got Eddie to thank for that – he was always telling me to be careful. I always thought he was being too cautious...'

The twins came and sat the other side of Jess. 'What's wrong, Auntie Jess?' asked Keira. 'Are you ill?'

'Nothing for you two to worry about, I'll be all right.' She managed a smile. She didn't want them knowing there were nasty people that came in the night and stole her things. They might have nightmares. 'I've gotta find somewhere else to live, that's all.'

'You can live with us!' shouted Kirsty, and the two of them started bouncing up and down on the sofa. 'She can live with us, can't she, Mummy?'

'For now – a week of you two and she'll be climbing the walls!'

Jess was settling down with her cup of tea when her mobile bleeped. She put her mug down and fished in her handbag for her mobile.

'Jessica? Giles.'

'Oh, hi.'

He was surprised to hear her tone. 'What's the matter?'

She moved into the hall so the twins couldn't hear her conversation. 'Well, when I got home I'd been burgled,' she said in a hushed voice.

'What? You've had a break-in?'

'Yeah. The police have been, but I don't hold out much hope.'

'Are you there now?'

'No, at Mandy's.' Oops! This could all get a bit crazy seeing as Giles thought Jess lived in Mandy's house.

'I'll come over. Tell me where it is.'

'No!' she blurted out, 'I'm fine, really. I told you, I can look after meself.'

There was obviously something she wasn't telling him. He would have to get to the bottom of this and soon. 'If you're sure?'

'Yeah, look, I'll sort it... with Mandy's help.'

'OK, I'll speak to you soon. Good luck.'

'Thanks.'

She put her mobile back in her handbag and went into the kitchen to find Mandy. 'That was Giles,' she said, with smug grin. 'God, have I got a lot to tell you. You won't believe it.'

'Try me.'

CHAPTER ELEVEN

Having slept in three different beds in as many days, Jess woke up and wondered where she was. As she slowly came to, there were a hundred and one things swimming around in her mind.

The first thing would be to tell Chris Jenkins about her break-in. She only hoped he would be understanding and maybe give her some time off to sort things out.

She needn't have worried.

'My dear girl!' he said when Jess arrived at Jenkins & Co. 'What a dreadful thing to come home to. Of course, take the day off and if there's anything I can do to help, don't hesitate to ask.'

'Thanks, Chris. There is one thing.'

'Yes?'

'Well, I'm sort of homeless now. I don't suppose there's any property to let on our books that I can rent?'

'I should think so. Have a word with Cynthia, she handles lettings.'

Jess went over to the desk where Cynthia sat tapping away at her computer. A big pile of papers was about to spill onto the floor and Jess hurriedly put her hands out to save them.

'Thanks, Jess. You OK?' she said, without looking up.

Jess didn't want to go over it all again but told her briefly about her terrible ordeal.

Cynthia stopped typing. 'You poor thing. I know someone that happened to only last week. Must be awful.'

'Yeah, not the best,' said Jess, wanting to put it behind her and move on. 'Chris said you might have a property for me to rent? I don't want much,' she said, wondering how much she would have to shell out, 'just a one-bedroom place.'

Cynthia looked at her computer screen, clicking the mouse. 'You're in luck! It just so happens we've been given these new instructions. Have a look.' She turned the screen towards Jess. A newly refurbished property flagged up onscreen. It looked ideal but could she afford it? She scrolled down to the proposed rent. Jess did a double-take – it was the same as what she'd been paying Rose.

'I'm going to view it later. I should think it'll soon be snapped up. Want to come with me?'

Jess brightened. 'Thanks, that would be fab. Where is it?'

'I think I've got some printed details here, somewhere.' Cynthia sorted through her pile of papers. 'Here we are.' She handed the sheet to Jess.

'Oh, Nunton Green. When can we go?'

'I'll just finish my coffee.'

Cynthia drove and as they looked for the property, Jess realised it was a stone's throw from Mandy's. She could walk there if she wanted and as they drew up outside the building she had a good feeling about it. She stood looking around while Cynthia found the keys and gathered her details. The property was in a smart cul-de-sac, a big improvement on Victoria Villas – not a wheelie bin in sight. There was a parade of shops nearby with a great-looking bakery, a small supermarket and a butcher. There were two pubs, one at each end of the green and what looked like a row of almshouses that lay back behind a brick wall. Like a little village in the middle of London.

Stepping through the shiny grey front door the sound of workmen sawing wood and some loud music echoed through the building.

'The flat downstairs is still being done up. The property used to be one house but needed a lot of TLC. A developer saw the potential and snapped it up,' said Cynthia.

They clonked up the wooden stairs and at the top, Jess pushed open the door onto the main living area. The smell of fresh paint and a bright airy space greeted her. 'Wow! This is cool.'

The apartment was completely refurbished. The light-coloured walls were exactly the shade Jess liked and the open-plan kitchenette was fitted with white shaker-style units and brand new appliances. Jess ran her hands over the imitation granite worktops and the white ceramic sink. A big double-glazed window allowed sunlight to flood the rest of the room and she could picture her furniture sitting on the laminate floor. When she walked through to the little bathroom her heart lifted at the sight of the cream tiles from floor to ceiling, a white suite and shower cubicle and shiny new taps. She examined the bedroom – beige carpet and another big window, the same as the living area. It was all too good to be true.

'I wouldn't mind a little place like this,' said Cynthia, looking around. 'I live with my mum since my old man ran off with my best friend. Luckily my kids are grown up with their own lives. You can't really go back home once you've left, you know; you get too set in your ways, but the longer I stay there the harder it is to leave.'

'Yeah, I can imagine but I don't even have that option.'

Cynthia was curious to know more about Jess; she always looked so confident. 'What about you? No parents, then?'

Jess shook her head.

'A husband or partner?'

'I've just met someone. He's a lawyer,' she said proudly. 'Early days, so we'll see.'

'What's his name?'

'Giles. Giles Morgan,' she said, suddenly enjoying the sound of his name on her tongue and turned to look out of the window once more.

Cynthia was surprised – her divorce was handled by one of his office staff and from what she'd seen of Giles Morgan, he was out of Jess's league. And married. 'I don't mean to pry but… have you known him long?'

'A couple of weeks. Why?'

'Oh, nothing. Forget it. It's none of my business.'

'I know he's married, if that's what you mean.'

'Really? Oh, well. I expect you know what you're doing.'

Jess thought she did. She certainly felt more confident after Saturday night. But there was still that underlying uncertainty that niggled away at her when she let it and she still felt guilty about Eddie. But she couldn't work Giles out. One minute he was all over her, and the next, he made her feel like she didn't exist. The Bitch's remark at the yacht club also kept coming back to her. '*He's no good with women, my dear.*'

Cynthia jogged Jess out of her reverie. 'Seen enough?'

'Oh, yeah. It's totally awesome. I love it!'

'Let's get back and get it sorted, then.'

Back at the office, Jess kept her fingers crossed as Cynthia went through the paperwork. Luckily, Eddie had always insisted Jess take out contents insurance on her flat. Once she'd put in her claim it should pay the deposit and the first few months' rent. Maybe even help some way towards new furniture.

'When can I move in?'

'As soon as we've completed the application forms and you've paid the deposit. Oh, and six months' rent in advance.'

Yes! She could just about scrape enough together. It might mean living on bread and cheese for a few weeks and no wine, but being burgled had been a blessing in disguise. She was on the threshold of a new life, she could feel it.

*

That evening, Jess went round to her old flat to salvage some of her furniture. As she let herself in it seemed alien to her – she couldn't imagine living there now.

Eddie was driving past when he noticed Jess's car parked outside and decided to pop in and surprise her. As he approached, he noticed a carpenter replacing the main front door. Not before time, he thought, the place had been in need of attention for years. But as he went upstairs he knew something was wrong. It was eerily quiet. He pushed open the door and was shocked to see Jess kneeling in the middle of the trashed room, sorting through some of her things.

'Christ! What happened?'

She looked round to see Eddie open-mouthed.

'Why didn't you phone me, Jess? I'm still your best friend. You know that.'

'Sorry, Eddie. I haven't had time.'

'State of this place...bloody hell.'

'Yeah, I know. I'm gutted.'

He bent down and picked up a shattered photo of the two of them together. As he did so a piece of broken glass slid out and fell to the floor, narrowly missing his foot. He swallowed hard. 'Bastards,' he muttered, and kicked the sofa. Jess had never witnessed such emotion in him before and felt part of his anger was directed at her. He made her uncomfortable. Eddie, sensing this, took a step back but all he wanted was to comfort her. 'Be careful Jess, the place is full of splintered glass. You shouldn't be kneeling down there.'

She immediately stood up and brushed off her knees.

'Look, if there's anything I can do..?'

'Well, now you mention it…you could help me move into me new apartment, if you like?'

Eddie's face lit up; he was only too pleased to be asked for help, but the word 'apartment' surprised him.

'When?'

'Soon as you like. I'm staying at Mandy's at the moment. She's been brilliant but I don't want to put on her.'

He blew out a sigh. 'You only had to ask, Jess. I'd have helped you. My sister's got a spare room.'

Jess thought about this. She didn't know his sister very well and since he and Jess had split up it would be too awkward for her to live there. 'Nah, it's OK. I'm sorted now anyway.'

Eddie nodded. 'Right, I'll have to organise a van. I'll get Andy.' He took out his mobile and turned his back to her. Forcing the lump even further down in his throat and suppressing the tears just under the surface, he rang Andy. 'Andy, it's me, mate. Any chance you can get the van over here one night?'

Jess continued sorting through her belongings and wondered how she was going to tell him about Giles. Maybe it could wait.

Eddie put his mobile back in his pocket, his shoulders hunched and still with his back to her. 'Yep. That's sorted. Tomorrow night OK?'

'Cool. Thanks, Eddie.'

He started towards the door.

'Don't you wanna see me new place? I'm going round there in a minute.'

He stopped dead. 'Nah, I'll leave it for now. See you later.' He ran down the stairs and out the main door. He was yesterday. He knew that now.

Jess felt awkward about the way Eddie had left so abruptly but at least she didn't have to phone him and ask for his help. Much better this way.

She was just checking to see if she had everything she needed when her mobile bleeped.

'Jessica, Giles here. How are you getting on?'

'Oh, not bad. I've got a new apartment; moving in tomorrow night.'

'Tomorrow? That was quick! Are you renting somewhere? How did you manage to get a removal firm so quickly?'

She wanted to laugh; he had no idea how she lived. 'Oh, I haven't got much furniture. I've got a friend with a van who's helping me.'

This all sounded very odd to Giles. The people he knew made such a fuss about moving.

'Jessica? Is there something you're not telling me?'

'What? Oh...' she knew she had to tell him – she couldn't keep it from him any longer. 'Yeah, it's just...I didn't tell you the truth about where I lived. I thought...'

He wasn't at all surprised.

'I didn't want you to see where it was,' she almost said, 'it's the pits' but settled for, 'it's not very nice.'

Giles sighed remembering his grandfather's speech. 'Jessica...' he wanted to say she needn't have worried, but she took his tone as a criticism.

'Look, I know I was out of order, but at least I've got a better place now. Being burgled did me a favour. It's near Mandy's.'

'This is all very confusing. Is that the place where Benson picked you up?'

'Yeah, that's where I'm staying at the moment.'

'Well, I'm glad we've got that cleared up. Maybe I can visit you in your new apartment when you're straight?'

'I'd like that,' but having said that, she couldn't picture him coming to visit.

He was feeling benevolent all of a sudden. 'Listen, you don't have to worry it's not in my league. For what it's worth, I hate that bloody place, but I'm sure you'll make yours very comfortable. Let me know when you've settled in.' Could he wait until then? He still wanted to take her to his boathouse and asked what she was doing next weekend.

'Oh, I've gotta work. Sorry.'

'But I thought you said you didn't have to work weekends now?'

'I know but this is a one-off.'

'In that case, perhaps you'd like to go out for a meal one evening?'

'Cool. I'd love to.'

'I'll speak to you soon.' He was looking forward to showing her off at one of his favourite restaurants in Greenwich but in the meantime he'd send her a bouquet of flowers to keep her interested. But where to? He came to the conclusion it would have to be Jenkins & Co.

No sooner had he put the phone down, Lydia rang.

'So... you *are* seeing that little tart! Really, Giles, I thought you had more sense.'

His stomach lurched. 'What are you talking about?'

'Oh, come on, I wasn't born yesterday.'

'Look, Lydia, we both know there's no point in carrying on with this charade. It's finished.'

Lydia laughed, scornfully. 'Ha! So it is true! You should have been more careful, darling, how foolish of you. You'll be hearing from my solicitor in due course.' She hung up.

Dammit and how dare she call him darling! He'd had a nasty feeling this might happen. He shouldn't have procrastinated; he should've divorced Lydia years ago. Instead, she could screw him to the ground for thousands, not to mention all the wagging tongues. He needed to avoid that at all costs. He began pacing the floor wondering what to do. He rang his father.

Jacob answered straight away. 'Giles! This is a nice surprise.'

'You won't say that when you know what it's about.'

'Oh? Why? What's the matter?'

Giles took a deep breath. 'I'm afraid Lydia suspects me of having an affair. She's divorcing me.'

There was silence at the other end. Giles knew how much his father revered Lydia – he only hoped Jacob would be sympathetic.

'And are you? Having an affair?'

Giles couldn't answer. He felt like he used to as a child, having a dressing down in front of his father. He was thankful he was on the phone and couldn't see him spitting tacks.

'When did this happen?'

Giles chewed his thumbnail. 'Oh, it's a recent thing. Lydia's just rung me, what am I going to do? She'll take me to the cleaners.'

'All right, all right, calm down. This needs some thought. In the meantime I'll talk to Henry.' Henry Bishop was Jacob's golf partner and the other half of Morgan Bishop. Together they had started the business and any occasion for them to meet up was eagerly jumped upon. 'Between the two of us I'm sure we can come up with something.'

'Thanks. *I* could talk to Henry – he's in tomorrow, isn't he?'

'No, no. Leave it to me. Pity. By the way; who's the other woman?'

'Her name's Jessica. You've seen her. She's the blonde that was helping to serve the meal on Saturday evening.'

Jacob hadn't taken much notice – Jess had kept out of his line of vision – but he did remember a blonde on the periphery now Giles came to mention her. He screwed up his nose. 'Ah, yes, that's right but I wouldn't have thought she was your type. All right for a one-night-stand but not serious material, surely?'

It came as no surprise to Giles that his father would see Jessica in this light but he couldn't think of anything to say in his or her defence.

'Have you known her long?'

'Three weeks.'

Jacob didn't like the sound of this one bit. His son could lose a large chunk of his fortune over a fling. 'Are you sure you know what you're doing?'

Giles wasn't at all sure but he was in it now, right up to his neck, whether he liked it or not. He still didn't know Jessica's true feelings for him and although he wanted Lydia out of his life, he would have preferred it on his own terms.

Jacob blew out a sigh. 'OK. Leave it with me.' He was amazed. He would like to know how this had all come about; it was totally out of character for Giles to behave in this way.

*

The next morning at Jenkins & Co. Jess was organising her work for the day when Chris walked over to her. 'You still OK to cover the viewings at Swallows Rise at the weekend?'

'Yeah, I'll have a go.'

'That's the spirit. I'll take you down there in a minute; I need to check on a few things and you can get the lie of the land.'

He went over to his desk and picked up the brochure. 'It's a select development of six new semi-detached houses. We're very lucky to have them on our books, Jess.'

Jess took the glossy brochure from him and flicked through it. *An exclusive but affordable development of six, three bedroom houses....* They looked amazing. She was looking forward to showing clients around and clinching deals.

A woman suddenly burst through the door with a huge bouquet. 'Flowers for Jessica Harvey?'

'That's me!' Jess ran over to relieve her of them. 'Wow! Thanks.' She read the message attached: "Jessica, looking forward to our next meeting, Giles." Her face lit up. She'd never seen such a ginormous bouquet – there were roses, carnations and lilies in all shades of pink, tied up in cellophane with a huge purple ribbon.

Chris and Cynthia had a pretty good idea who they were from. Chris wanted to warn her not to get involved with Giles Morgan but it looked like he was too late. He was becoming fond of Jess, in a fatherly way, but decided not to press the matter. 'You can put them in water in the kitchen sink for now, Jess.' He walked towards the door. 'When you're ready.'

Jess hurriedly did as he suggested then went to join him in the car.

On the journey he asked why she had answered his advert. She told him it was because she thought she'd blown it with Giles. A pity she hadn't, he thought; he would like to see her in a proper relationship, with someone like his son, for instance. He quite fancied her as his daughter-in-law.

'How old are you, Jess?'

'Coming up for the big 3-0 in a couple o' weeks.'

'Really? You don't look it.'

'Thanks, but I feel like life is passing me by sometimes.'

'What makes you say that?'

'Oh, I dunno. A lot of girls I went to school with are married with kids.'

'You mustn't worry about that. You've still got plenty of time.' His son was thirty- two and felt the same way; pity he couldn't get them together.

'You're about the same age as my son, Mark.'

'Oh? What does he do?'

'He's a ladies hairdresser, I think I told you? He didn't want to go into the family business. He's got his own shop called Razor Sharp. It's only a small concern, but he's doing very well.'

Jess knew the place; it was in a small parade of shops on Brandon Street. From the outside it looked quite smart.

'I'll have to pay him a visit. I can't go back to Top to Toe after getting the bullet.' Oops! How did that slip out?

Chris stopped the car at the traffic lights and looked at her. 'You didn't tell me.'

'Yeah, well... it was after I knew I got this job; I'd had enough of Liz one day and just lost it.'

'I see.'

Cars were beeping so he put the car in gear and set off again. He chewed over this revelation in his mind – maybe there was no need to worry where Giles Morgan was concerned, after all. Jess didn't seem the type to stand for any nonsense.

They turned into a small cul-de-sac and Chris parked on the little gravel drive in front of the show home. Jess thought he'd made a mistake; this development didn't look anything like the one in the brochure. Swallows Rise had a play ground squashed up at one end and the houses looked a lot smaller than in the photos.

Chris unlocked the door and sat in one of the armchairs in the front room. He checked his emails on his lap top and urged Jess to have a look round.

She went upstairs first and was shocked to find the bedrooms were tiny – just enough room to walk around the double bed in the so-called master bedroom and the en-suite was so small Jess imagined it would be like having a shower in a telephone box. The other double bedroom was just as small and the single was more suited to a dressing room or an office. The bathroom consisted of a wash hand basin the size of a mixing bowl, a half size bath with an overhead shower and a tiny WC, all crammed together. Downstairs, the kitchen-diner was just about big enough for the small table and chairs wedged into the corner and in the lounge the three piece suite took up the whole of the room. In fact, it made Jess's little studio flat look quite spacious.

She looked out the window – the 'low-maintenance' back garden was paved with a small shed but what the hell would you put in that? There certainly wasn't any need for garden machinery or tools in a garden of this size. Low-maintenance was just another word for non-existent, thought Jess. No garage and only one allotted parking space in front of the property. These houses certainly weren't all they were cracked up to be. The brochure lied. Jess turned round to face Chris.

'Well? What do you think?'

Jess decided to be diplomatic. 'They're a bit on the small side.'

'Ah, yes but they're aimed at the first time buyer. Starter homes. Two of them are on a part buy, part rent basis. They'll sell like hot cakes,' he said, dismissively.

*

On Tuesday evening as promised, Eddie and Andy turned up outside Jess's old flat with the van. Eddie went upstairs to find Jess and couldn't help noticing the over-the-top bouquet of flowers lying on the floor next to her handbag. While Jess was in the kitchen he quickly looked to see who they were from. Oh, so... Giles was it? He had a pretty good idea he was the same person she'd had lunch with a couple of weeks ago.

Andy grabbed his arm. 'Come on, mate. The sooner we're done, the sooner we can get in the boozer.'

The two guys set about loading the good furniture into the van. Eddie's eyes fell upon the trash in middle of the floor and felt his past life had been discarded with it. While he was helping Andy secure the furniture in the back of the van he noticed Jess laid the bouquet of flowers carefully in her car. She turned to go back inside and called to Eddie, 'I'm going back up to check you've got it all.'

Eddie followed her upstairs and stood beside her. The transformation was sickening. It felt unreal standing together in this room that had once been their home.

'So,' said Eddie, 'end of an era.'

Jess nodded, lost for words.

'We had some good times in here, Jess. Pity it had to come to this.'

She looked at him. 'Don't be sad, Eddie. At least we've got the memories.'

'Shame it's not more. I do miss you, Jess.' He went to hug her but she stepped back and tossed her hair over her shoulders.

'I know, but you can always pop round, you know.'

'Nah, it's all right. I couldn't hack it if I burst in and found you with... someone else. I don't think I'm ready for that.'

'Don't worry, I can't see him coming round here too often.'

Was he in with a chance then? 'Well, you know where I am if you need me. Anytime...'

'Oi, you coming?' Andy shouted from downstairs, 'we're wasting valuable drinking time.'

Eddie started towards the stairs. 'I'll see you round the new place then.'

She handed him the keys and watched him run downstairs. From the window she saw him saunter to the van, his head hung low. After making a final check, Jess mentally said goodbye to the old place and sat in her car with a mixture of emotions. Yes it was a sad end to her flat in Victoria Villas but she was looking forward to making her new home in Nunton Green.

Outside her apartment, Jess arrived to see Andy sitting in the van on his own. He wound down the window and shouted, 'Tell him to get a move on, will yer? Dunno what's keepin' 'im.'

They had made short work of unloading her few items of furniture and she found Eddie upstairs, hovering, unsure whether to go or stay. 'It's nice, Jess.'

'Yeah, better than in the old place.'

He nodded. 'Think you'll be happy here?'

'Yeah, Mandy's only up the road. I've never had that, you know? A friend nearby.'

What about me, he wanted to say, but instead said, 'Well, I'll be off, then.'

'Yeah. Thanks, Eddie.'

He managed a smile. 'Let me know how you get on?'

She smiled back. 'Yeah, cool.'

The van roared away. Jess stood in the centre of the room and turned full circle to survey her new abode. Her new landlord had thought of everything. There was even a coat rack on the landing wall, a first aid cabinet in the bathroom and a big airing cupboard she'd failed to notice before. She felt at home already, her own things dotted about and some new furniture and she'd be happy. She was even looking forward to doing a bit of entertaining now Mandy, Trevor and the twins were nearby.

After putting the bouquet in water and standing the vase on the windowsill, she made a cup of tea, kicked off her shoes and tucked her legs under her on the sofa. Her attention was drawn to a stain on the arm where Eddie had upset a glass of beer one night.

She ran her hand over it and smiled, remembering how it had happened. She had half a mind to call him back.

CHAPTER TWELVE

Jess noticed a neighbour's curtain twitch as she sat in the back seat of the Mercedes and felt smug.

As before, Benson escorted her silently into the lift and up to the apartment. Was it only two weeks ago that she had first set foot in here? It seemed much longer. She watched as Benson took her holdall down the hall and assumed he must be heading for the master bedroom. Progress at last.

She entered the lounge. Giles greeted her with a kiss and stood back to admire her. She had chosen her little black dress and her black killer heels. 'You look stunning.'

She glowed. This was more like it.

'I trust you received the flowers?'

'Yeah, thanks, they're gorgeous.'

'Glad you like them.' He walked over to the cocktail cabinet. 'Drink?'

'Please.' Jess saw his whisky on the side table and realised he had started without her.

As Giles opened a chilled bottle of Pinot Grigio, Jess's eyes scanned the room with renewed interest and she found she was even more curious about the large oil painting in the heavy gilt frame. She went to the mantelpiece to take a closer look.

Giles handed her the glass of wine and gave the painting a cursory glance. 'I've never liked it. It's supposed to be Coverdale, Yorkshire, but I find it dark and depressing.'

She moved closer trying to pick out a few details. 'I've never been to Yorkshire. I don't know why, but I feel I know this place.'

'Oh?'

'Yeah, I think my Nan mentioned something about a painting belonging to our family years ago, but it got lost. She said that picture was of somewhere in Yorkshire.'

Giles thought he ought to show an interest. 'Really? Well, this one's Lydia's; she brought it with her when we got married,' Giles said dismissively. *Damn the painting and damn Lydia!* 'I would have preferred to see a galleon in full sail, or a clipper ship, but Lydia insisted on this one. I might do something about it one day.'

Jess noticed that he had some smaller paintings of naval scenes on the other walls.

'At least it's marginally better than all this modern art rubbish,' he said, remembering Ted's attempts.

'Oh? You don't you like contemporary art, then?'

'No. Monkeys could do a better job.'

She smiled but kept her opinions to herself. She liked all kinds of art but it was out of her reach. But this painting held a fascination for her that she couldn't explain. She stood in front of it studying the figure lying under the tree. She couldn't quite make it out. Was it a boy or a girl? There were some cows in the distance and the heavy grey clouds looked full of rain.

Giles shook her out of her reverie. 'Well, if you're ready? We can walk to the restaurant; it's not far and it's a lovely evening.'

When they reached the Terrace Restaurant Jess's killer heels were living up to their name. She needed to kick them off but after looking around at the upper-crust diners enjoying their evening she decided against it. The waitress came forward and showed them to their table in the Piano Bar.

'Nice in 'ere, innit?' said Jess, and wished she had remembered to put on her posh accent.

Feeling an affinity with Henry Higgins in *My Fair Lady,* Giles hoped Jess's remark had fallen on deaf ears.

The waitress handed them each a menu and asked what they would like to drink. Jess managed to kick off her shoes under the table, rubbed her feet together and sighed inwardly. She asked for a glass of Pinot Grigio. Giles had his usual whisky.

A pianist dressed in a tuxedo took his place at the shiny baby grand and proceeded to play an Irving Berlin medley. Jess glanced around and felt she'd 'arrived'. So this is how the rich lived? She half expected to see someone famous here tonight.

The waitress brought their drinks. Giles took a mouthful of whisky and sat back listening to the music. 'Did you hear my father and Lydia playing on Saturday evening?'

'I thought I heard something but Becks and me were flat out.' Jess's mind was transported back to that evening and the summer house. 'Do you think she twigged?'

Giles knew exactly what she was referring to but he didn't want to talk about Lydia – she always seemed to upstage him even when she was absent. He hadn't intended to let Jessica into his private affairs either but he needed to confide in her.

'I'm afraid so. She's doing her damndest to make my life hell.'

'Blimey! What will you do?'

'Well, she thinks she's got the upper hand but she's in for a shock.'

Jess's big-eyed gaze sent an exquisite feeling running through his body; it was difficult to keep his mind focused. 'She's divorcing me, or thinks she is. My father and Henry are doing all they can before Lydia ruins me.'

'Bitch!'

Silence engulfed the restaurant. Even the pianist had stopped playing at that precise moment.

Giles's quick eyes darted around the room. 'Sssh! I'm trying to keep this under wraps.'

'Sorry,' whispered Jess, 'me and my big mouth.'

The waitress emerged hoping to hear a juicy bit of gossip but Giles gave her one of his glares.

'Ready to order?' she asked.

Jess couldn't make up her mind, there were so many lovely dishes to choose from, but she plumped for the lamb shank tagine with roasted vegetables and minted cous cous. Giles said he'd have the chicken Caesar salad – it would be easier to digest given his rising bile that Lydia was causing once again. She had to spoil everything. The sooner his father and Henry could send her packing the better.

The waitress took their order and asked if they would like anything else to drink?

'I'd love another glass of wine,' said Jess.

'Make it a bottle of your finest Pinot Grigio, would you?' said Giles.

Jess glowed.

'How did the move go?' asked Giles.

Eddie flashed into her mind. She didn't want to talk about it. 'Oh, fine. It was soon done.'

But Giles dug in a bit further. 'Who helped you?'

Uh-oh. Jess didn't know how to refer to Eddie, but in the end she settled for 'just a friend'.

'Have you known him long?'

'Yeah, ages.'

From Giles's expression she realised he wanted more.

'Look. I might as well get this out o' the way…'

The waitress brought the bottle of wine and started to pour. Giles snapped, 'Leave it, would you?'

The waitress scowled at him and stormed off.

Jess took a deep breath and reached for the bottle. Giles snatched it from her and poured her a glass. 'Well?'

'We used to live together.'

'Ah.'

She nodded. 'Yeah,' she took a mouthful of wine, hoping it would give her some courage, 'but we split up a couple of months ago.'

'I see. Was it mutual?'

She nodded and averted her eyes. It was a lie. Eddie had been really cut up. He still made her feel uncomfortable, especially last night.

'How long were you together?'

'God, you're asking a lot of questions.'

'Yes, but I think you owe it to me.'

She didn't think she owed him anything but decided to keep a lid on it. She didn't want to cause a scene. 'Almost four years, if you must know. Since we're on the subject, how long have you and the 'bitch-from-hell' been together?'

'Can we drop it? People are staring.'

The waitress came back with their food. Giles wasn't at all hungry; he felt like walking out. He picked at the salad and watched Jessica tucking into her food. She puzzled him. She obviously had a totally different upbringing from him, but until she opened her mouth no one would ever know. She walked tall and was well turned out and something else he couldn't quite put his finger on. Breeding? No. That really was a step too far. Or was it?

It looked like they were here for the duration so he decided to lighten the mood. 'How's the lamb? Good as yours?'

She rolled her eyes. The joke had been done to death, unlike the lamb. 'It's delicious. I love lamb; it used to be a real treat when I was growing up. Me Nan used to tell me it was lamb I was eating, even if it wasn't, just to get me to eat. But my dad used to get cross when I picked at my food. He'd say "eat it or wear it!" Shelley wasn't so fussy; she ate whatever was put in front of her.'

'Oh, so you have a sister? Where does she live?'

Jess sighed. 'Australia. She went back-packing with her boyfriend when I was eighteen and ended up living there.'

He had to know more. 'And your parents?'

'Both dead.'

He was stunned at the way she'd blurted it out. He put his knife and fork down and waited for her to show some emotion, but thankfully, not being able to empathise with people, Giles was relieved at the way she was being amazingly blasé.

'That's why I'm so used to looking after meself.'

Giles was silent while he processed this information.

'And you', she ventured, 'any brothers and sisters?'

He drained his glass. 'No. I'm an only child.'

Now it was her turn. 'Oh? Why's that?' she smiled, 'no, don't tell me – they took one look at you and decided against it!'

A half smile. 'My mother had such a bad time, she nearly died. She was advised not to have any more children.'

Jess's heart went out to Morwenna who she wished she'd had the chance to meet on Saturday night. 'Poor woman. Would you have liked a brother or sister?'

'Not really.'

'Why's that?'

'Look, leave it, OK?'

Jess felt she'd overstepped the mark so she shut up. What was she thinking? She'd have to watch her tongue in future if she wanted this to work. But she was getting a bit fed up with his attitude – he was always so serious. She couldn't get a titter out of him, unlike Eddie.

They finished their meal in silence.

The pianist came to the end of the Irving Berlin medley and Jess applauded him. Some of the other diners followed her lead. After taking a bow, he announced he was now going to play a Beatles medley.

'He's gradually getting more up to date,' said Giles, 'Not my era but I still like them.'

'Me too. Me Dad used to get the record player out on a Saturday night and the Beatles always went on.' Jess remembered *Money*' being one of his favourites but she kept it to herself.

The waitress came to take their plates and ask if they would like any dessert. Jess said she would like the pear in red wine with raspberry sorbet.

'Have you got any chocolate tipsy tart?' asked Giles.

Jess gave a snort and clapped her hand over her mouth. 'Sorry.'

The waitress looked from one to the other. 'That's not on the menu, is it?' She took it from Jess. 'No, I didn't think so. Death by Chocolate?' asked the waitress.

'OK, that sounds good, thanks.'

The waitress hurried away.

'What's so funny?' asked Giles.

'Last Saturday – I was trying so hard to keep out of the dining room in case Lydia saw me… we had such a laugh. I nearly died when she came into the kitchen.'

Giles was immediately reminded of their late night liaison but was now regretting his impulsive behaviour. If he hadn't taken Jessica into the summer house she would still be his secret. If only he'd controlled himself. He wondered how he'd been so reckless. Now he was paying for it. Was Jessica worth it? He wasn't sure

Their desserts arrived. The waitress set them down and went to take another order.

Giles picked up his cake fork, put it down again and looked straight into Jessica's eyes. 'The truth is – I think I'm falling in love with you.'

She saw all her privileged future flash before her eyes. It was more than a dream come true but she didn't want to give him the satisfaction so she smiled sweetly and looked down at her hands.

Giles pushed his Death by Chocolate around his plate. 'I'm sorry. I shouldn't have said anything. It's too soon.'

'No. I'm fine with it. Really.'

He suddenly needed some fresh air. 'If you've finished, we'll have a wander back to the apartment.'

As they walked along by the river Jess was deep in thought. She forgot about her sore feet. It could all just work out for her, but shouldn't she be true to herself? Eddie invaded her thoughts again.

What would he think? Did it matter? For some reason it did. But she was on the brink of having the life she'd always wanted.

*

At 7am Jess left Giles in bed and went to find the kitchen to make some breakfast. As she opened the door and turned on the lights the huge white expanse hit her like a lightening bolt. She stood for a moment taking it all in, the long run of shiny white units with real granite worktops, the island and the black leather bar stools. Spotting the big red Aga she lifted one of the hotplate covers to feel the heat rising from it. She rubbed her hands together – she'd never cooked on a range. Coffee first – there was a red state-of –the-art coffee maker on the worktop, she found the ground coffee and put some on to brew. Next, she found a frying pan, some eggs, flour and milk and proceeded to make some pancakes. She was enjoying this.

She was arranging it all on a tray when she heard the door.

It was Joan. 'Oh, dear, dear me! What are you doing? Here, let me,' she put down her shopping bags and hung up her jacket.

'It's OK. I can manage,' said Jess.

Joan looked at the pancakes and tutted. 'Mr Giles always has muesli and fresh fruit for breakfast, dear.'

'Never mind, I'll surprise him,' said Jess and took the tray along to the bedroom.

Giles watched lazily from the bed as Jess's white silky robe slipped to reveal her smooth, shapely legs as she bent to put down the tray.

He reached out and grabbed her by the wrist. 'Come back to bed.'

She broke free of his grasp. 'I can't…I'll be late. You wouldn't want me to lose me job, would you?'

He didn't care and food was far from his thoughts.

She gave him a quick kiss on the lips. 'Eat up. I've gotta love and leave you.' She gobbled up the last of her pancake and went to take a shower. Giles watched through the crack of the door. He shivered with excitement as she let her robe fall to the floor.

Stepping into the shiny double cubical she gloried in the luxury power shower and briefly imagined Eddie soaping her body.

Giles slipped in beside her.

She was startled. 'Arrgh! What you doing?'

He silenced her with a kiss and slid his hands over her silky skin. He wanted to take her there and then.

'Giles!'

'What's the matter? I'll run you to work. It's not a problem.'

She answered him with a hard stare. His ardour was immediately dampened.

*

Screeching to a halt outside the show home at Swallows Rise, Jess noticed a couple with their two young children waiting outside. She was surprised to find it was Mr and Mrs Brown from the two up, two down. Their little boy was splashing about in the puddles and Jess made a mental note to mention this to Chris; the footpath would have to be finished off.

She jumped out of her car, grabbed her laptop and her paperwork and shook hands with Mr Brown who reluctantly reciprocated. 'I hope I haven't kept you waiting long.'

He answered her with a just-get-on-with-it look. Jess let them in but before she had a chance to organise her files, the little boy started jumping about on the beige carpet with his muddy shoes.

'I'm sorry,' said Jess, 'but can you take his shoes off? We're trying to keep the floors clean.'

'Is that really necessary?' asked his father

Judging by the state of their own place, thought Jess, the child wasn't used to being told but she tried to be diplomatic. She bent down to the little boy, 'If you let me take your shoes off, I'll give you a chocolate. How's that?'

His face lit up but his father protested. 'We don't agree with bribes.'

'Well, in that case Mr Brown, you'll have to wait outside with your son while I show your wife round.'

Mrs Brown smiled to herself; it obviously struck a chord with her but her husband was incensed. 'I don't believe this. I'll be writing to your Mr Jenkins; I don't like your attitude.' Nevertheless, he took the child and went to sit in the car.

'Would you like to see upstairs first?' asked Jess.

Mrs Brown, complete with toddler-on-hip, nodded and followed Jess. She was very impressed with the level of workmanship but thought the bedrooms were much too small. She was looking for a larger three-bed property but said her husband was curious about Swallows Rise. 'I told him they weren't big enough for us but he wouldn't listen, said he wanted a new-build.'

Jess wanted to agree with her but instead pointed out the built-in cupboards and the amount of storage space. After all, she was supposed to be selling these properties. Downstairs, Mrs Brown said she couldn't imagine three small boys running about in there. 'And the garden's like a postage stamp, nowhere for Thomas to play.'

'There's a playground at the end,' offered Jess, 'he'd be nice and safe and you and your husband could enjoy some peace and quiet in the secluded garden.'

'I'm sorry, I know you're only doing your job but I'll see what Dennis says.' Mrs Brown went out to the car where her husband was trying to keep Thomas amused. She poked her head in the open window. 'See what you think, darling.'

'I'm not going back in there. That damned slip of a girl – who does she think she is? Come on. Let's go.'

Mrs Brown turned to Jess with a shrug and got back in the car.

Jess went to switch on the coffee maker and organise her paperwork, hoping there wouldn't be too many families like the Browns to contend with.

Chris rang. 'Jess. Just checking you're OK. Got everything you need?'

'I think so.'

'Good. Had anyone round to view?'

'Yep. Mr and Mrs Brown from the skanky terraced... Oops, sorry. I didn't mean...'

'Oh? That's surprising. I would have thought Swallows Rise was out of their reach. Anyone else?'

Phew! thought Jess, 'Nope, not yet.'

'Well, good luck. I'm at the Bermondsey office if you need me.'

'Cool. Oh, before you go...'

'Yes?'

'Mr Brown might be phoning you. He's not happy about me telling his son to take his muddy shoes off; he was jumping about in the puddles at the front when I got here.'

There was a pause while Chris pictured the situation. It amused him. 'I shouldn't worry about that, Jess. You did the right thing,' but as an afterthought, 'Have a word with the site manager, if he's about; something needs to be done about those puddles.'

Jess was feeling so smug after that she could cope with anything. Except... Boredom.

Six cups of coffee later there hadn't been a single viewing, not even a phone call. She'd done all the jobs including tidying the desk and washing up and as usual in these situations, her mind began to wander. When should she see Mandy? And then there was Razor Sharp. Jess needed to get her hair done and made a note to ring Mark Jenkins and book an appointment.

As for Giles, the luxury life definitely appealed but every time she was in bed with him something niggled at her. And what about Mandy, Trevor and the twins? She couldn't imagine Giles with them. Then there was that painting. She didn't know why it intrigued her so; it was only a distant memory. Maybe Shelley would know? Oh my God, Shelley! She still hadn't told her she'd moved. Jess took out her laptop and rushed off an email to her.

Four o'clock couldn't come soon enough. She drove home, put the kettle on and rang Giles. No answer. Three guesses as to where he was then.

CHAPTER THIRTEEN

Giles was adamant the Lydia incident wasn't going to stop him attending his club. He hadn't ventured in there since his birthday but he decided to brave it and sod the consequences. He was having withdrawal symptoms.

As soon as he arrived Dickie and Ron pounced on him. 'Giles, old boy,' started Dickie, 'long time, no see. How's that little filly you brought with you last time, the pretty blonde?'

'She's fine, thanks, Dick.' Giles was relieved Dickie had not mentioned Lydia's outburst.

'Do I detect something?' asked Ron, looking sideways at Giles.

'What?'

'Well, you look… different.'

'Do I?'

'I should say so. What do you think, Dick?'

'Nudge, nudge, wink, wink, eh? You're in there, old boy. Make the most of it, I should.'

Giles ignored these remarks. He wasn't about to share his private life with these two; it would be all round the club in no time. He went over to the bar and ordered a drink for himself and one each for Dickie and Ron. Changing the subject he said, 'I've come to see if there's anything going on this weekend, any racing?'

'I think there's some social event or other; a Booze Cruise, or some such,' said Dickie. 'Why? Thinking of taking what's-her-name?'

Giles ignored the question.

Ron looked at Dickie then at Giles. 'We've got a race tomorrow if you want to join us?'

'That would be great, thanks.'

Dickie tried again. 'Bringing the blonde?'

Giles took a long swig of his scotch. 'Her name's Jessica. And no, she's working.'

'Oh? That's a shame. Thought she might liven things up a bit.'

Giles wasn't going to volunteer any more information. So, Jessica had caused a bit of a stir, had she? He could understand why, but his first love was sailing and he was going to make damned sure he made the most of it this weekend. The weather looked set to remain sunny with a slight breeze. Perfect.

*

Jess was just settling down to a cosy night in when Mandy rang. 'Hi, Jess, fancy slumming it? Connie and Sarah's idea – Saucy Meg's. I thought you'd like to go, seeing as they haven't seen you for ages.'

'OK, cool.'

'Not seeing Giles tonight, then?'

'Doesn't look like it.'

'Thought you might like bronco burgers and ribs for a change instead of pretty picture food?''

'OK. What time?'

'About eight, see you down there.'

Saucy Meg's was a Western-style bar with food to match. Jess never thought she'd say this, but it would make a welcome change from the restaurants Giles favoured with their nouvelle cuisine and Michelin stars. That was all very well but she had to be on her best behaviour all the time. Apart from the evening with Becks at the Morgan's, life had become a little too serious of late. She would have to scrape by for the rest of the week, money was tight since her move, but she was looking forward to having a laugh and letting her hair down tonight. Out came her Levis, her cowboy boots and her suede jacket with the fringe, all topped off with her Stetson raked at a jaunty angle. She surveyed her image in the mirror and punched the air. 'Yesss! Get in.'

Saucy Meg's was jumping to the beat when Jess arrived. Apart from the music it was like walking onto a film set of a Western saloon. She walked over to where Mandy, Connie and Sarah were sitting. 'Hi, all right?'

Sarah nodded, her mouth full of spicy rib. 'Mm, this is good,' she said, wiping her mouth with a tissue. 'Where you been hiding?'

Jess answered with a shrug.

'What about this Giles, then?'

'Yeah, he's cool.'

'And the job?' asked Connie, biting into her burger, the sauce squelching out.

'It's good, much better than having to put up with Liz's old ducks.'

Mandy looked up from her plate of ribs. 'You wanna get some of this, Jess, before it all goes. It's really good.'

Jess went to the bar and ordered some hot spicy ribs and fries, bought a coke and went back to sit with her friends to catch up with the latest antics at Top to Toe. The waitress brought her food over and she soon got stuck in. Mandy was right – it was good. Jess had missed all this – she'd forgotten what it was like to hang out with her own crowd without having to watch what she said and how she behaved.

The evening was hotting up with shouts of Yee, Har! and line-dancing to '*Achy Breaky Heart*.' What would Giles think if he saw her now? She couldn't picture him in a place like this. Definitely not his scene. She looked around in case Eddie had shown up but he hadn't. It had been a long time since he and Jess had had a night out in Saucy Meg's – it used to be one of their favourite haunts.

Mandy and Connie finished their meals and went to join in the line-dance. Jess watched until Sarah nudged her, nearly sending a mouthful of rib across her face.

'Hey, don't look now. Over there, eye candy!'

Two guys were eyeing them up from across the bar. From the edge of her vision Jess noticed one was tall, dark and full-of-himself, his mate a bit shorter with fair hair and a bit worse for drink. 'Don't fancy yours much!'

'Oh, thanks. I saw him first, and anyway, you've already got one.'

'So?'

'Yeah, but from what I hear this Giles is a bit of a catch.'

'Yeah, minted,' said Jess, without changing her expression.

The taller of the two guys, in double denim and cowboy boots, flashed them a toothpaste grin and sauntered over looking straight at Jess. 'Hi, can I get you gals a drink?'

He was cool and he knew it, as if he'd just stepped out of *The Magnificent Seven*.

Jess played up to him. 'Well, thank you, kind sir.'

'What's your poison, lady?' he said, staring at her.

Sarah butted in. 'Mine's a bourbon.'

His eyes never left Jess. They were all over her like a searchlight. 'And yours?'

'Vodka and Red Bull, please.'

'Yee, har!'

All right, he was over-the-top but Jess didn't care. She thought it might be a laugh to play along with his theatrical antics. He went to the bar and Sarah bent closer to Jess. 'Is he for real?'

'Watch out! Here comes his mate.'

'Howdy there, girls,' he slurred, and sat next to Sarah who gave him a wide berth.

His mate came back with the drinks, handed them round and pulled up a stool. 'I see you've met Ben. I'm Danny. Come here often?'

Jess grinned. 'I can't believe you said that.'

'Yeah, I know, right? But seriously, I haven't seen you in here before.'

'It's been a while.'

Mandy and Connie came back from the floor. Mandy lifted her eyebrows at Jess and tilted her head questioningly in Danny's direction

Danny stood up and tipped his Stetson. 'Hi, I'm Danny, pleased to make your acquaintance, ma'am.'

Ben knocked over a stool and staggered outside.

Mandy tried not to laugh. Danny was obviously used to playing to an audience. 'Are you into amateur dramatics by any chance?'

'Yep. How'd you guess?' he flashed that smile again. 'I belong to the local outfit down at New Cross.'

'You really get into it, don't yer?'

'Yeah, why not? Real life's a bit dull ain't it?' Jess couldn't agree, not after the last few weeks she'd had.

'What do you do job-wise,' asked Jess.

'I sell insurance, if you must know.'

'Ah, OK. Ever thought of going on the stage for a living?' Jess and Mandy stifled a chuckle.

'Huh. I wish, but it don't pay the bills, lady.' He turned to Jess. 'Why don't you join us one night? See what you think? It's a fun way of getting to be someone else for a few hours.'

'I'm quite happy with the person I am, thanks. Anyway, I'm a bit slammed at the minute.'

'Shame.'

Sarah saw her chance. 'We could both join, Jess. What about it?'

'Yeah, why not?' said Danny, 'we're always looking for fresh talent.'

Jess shot Sarah a look 'Nah, it's OK. You go ahead.'

Danny tried again. 'It's great fun, Jess. I know you'd enjoy it.'

How the hell did *he* know what she'd enjoy, thought Jess. She told him she'd think about it, left him with Sarah and went to join Mandy and Connie who had gone back up for another dance.

As the evening wore on, the girls had a laugh together with Danny periodically trying to muscle in. By 11 o'clock Mandy was anxious about the baby sitter and Connie admitted she needed to leave, too, which left Sarah feeling like the third wheel. It was now obvious she wasn't going to get anywhere with Danny. 'Can I share a taxi with you, Con?'

'Sure, no probs,' said Connie, and all three got up to leave.

'See you tomorrow, Jess,' asked Mandy, 'Sunday lunch?'

'Oh, I can't, I'm working. Anyway, it's my turn. Come round to me next Sunday.'

'That'd be great, thanks, if you don't mind the tribe descending on you?'

'Cool. I'll ring you.'

Now Danny had Jess all to himself he continued to try and win her round but just as she was reconsidering joining the am dram group, Ben came staggering back completely wasted and fell against Jess, spilling his beer all down her jeans.

'Hey! Watch out you idiot!' Danny turned to Jess who stood up and was frantically trying to mop up her jeans with a tissue. 'I'm really sorry about him. He never knows when he's had enough.'

'Look, I'm done OK?' All she wanted was to jump in a nice hot shower.

'Right, don't forget. We meet every Thursday. See you down there?'

Jess dashed out through the saloon doors and jumped into a waiting taxi, leaving Danny staring after her.

CHAPTER FOURTEEN

The next day at 11 o'clock, a young couple burst into the show home at Swallows Rise. They had been to view one of the houses the previous week and had put down a deposit, so today they wanted to take another look and check out some measurements. Also, the girl had changed her mind about the tiles for the kitchen and wanted some advice. Jess was itching to get onto it but couldn't find the paperwork on their property.

The guy sighed heavily and crossed his arms. 'Isn't there someone in charge? Where's Jenkins?'

'I'm sorry, he's not here today. How can I help?'

'Well, can we change the order for the kitchen tiles or not?'

'I'm sure you can.'

'Look, we're coughing up good money; we need to know what we're getting.'

'Of course,' said Jess, trying to keep a lid on the situation. 'I'd be the same. If you'll bear with me, I'll give Mr Jenkins a ring. Can I take your name?'

'Carson,' said the man and started pacing the floor putting Jess on edge but his girlfriend was blissfully unaware and began examining the swatch samples for the sofas.

Chris answered. 'Jess. What can I do for you?'

'I've got a Mr Carson here. He wants to know if they can change the order for the tiles.'

'Ah, yes, I remember. Nice young couple...put a deposit down on number three. Tell them it's not a problem; the order hasn't gone through yet. Show them the Fired Earth brochure; you'll find it under the coffee table along with the Farrow and Ball colour chart and the Sanderson fabrics. Anything else?'

'Yes. I'd like the paperwork on their property, please.'

'Should be in the back of the folder, on your desk.'

Jess glowed at the sound of *your desk*. She found it. 'Yep, got it. Thanks Chris.'

She turned to Mr Carson. 'If you'd like to take a seat, I'll get you a cup of freshly brewed coffee while you browse.'

His girlfriend's ears pricked up. 'Ooh, lovely,' she said, and curled up on the sofa still thumbing through the swatches.

Mr Carson stared at Jess. 'So, what's the answer?'

Jess ignored him. She thought him rather rude and turned to his girlfriend. 'Milk and sugar?'

'Just milk, thanks. I'm Terri by the way.'

'Jess.'

He tried again. 'I asked you a question. Can we or can we not change the order?'

'Of course you can. If you'd like to choose an alternative I'll make a note of the new instructions.' Jess handed him the brochure.

He snatched it from her and sat down next to his girlfriend. 'Well, I hope you get it right. We don't want any cock-ups.'

Jess was determined to stay calm. She turned her attention to Terri and put the coffee down in front of her. 'Here we are. Help yourself to milk. Now, how can I help you?'

'Well, I've changed my mind.'

'Yeah, why not,' said Jess, with a forced smile at Mr Carson.

'Yes. I wanted brown but now I think they'll be too dark. I think white would be better.'

Jess went to take the Fired Earth brochure from Mr Carson who glared at her. 'Sorry. Can I see?' Jess continued, 'There's an awful lot of white in there already; I think you need a colour, Terri. How about these lovely blue ones?'

'Blue? I'd never have thought of that. Not very 'on trend' is it?'

Jess showed her the current *House & Garden* magazine. 'Well, I think they'd look good with these pink ones.'

Mr Carlson huffed. 'Pink?' he was now red faced, 'Poxy pink? It's a kitchen, not a tart's bedroom!'

Both women ignored him and Jess showed Terri another page from *House & Garden*. They took it through to the kitchen.

'Ooh, do you know, I think you're right,' said Terri, 'I would never have thought... but with the white and a bit of pink, it works! Yes, lovely.'

'Right, that's settled then.' Mr Carson was now in the doorway, hopping from one foot to the other, looking at his watch. 'Happy love?'

'Yes, very. Thanks, Jess.'

'Cool. Anything else?'

'Well, now you come to mention it, I don't suppose you've got any ideas for curtains to go with that?'

'Ooh. Let's see. We've got a great brochure for blinds. They might be better,' Jess went back to the coffee table.

Mr Carlson glared at Jess for prolonging the situation but she continued to help Terri and showed her the mood board she had created for her own apartment, if and when she had the money. 'How about something like this?'

'Ooh, yes. They'd look great. What do you think, darling?'

He was ready to agree to anything. The pub was open and he gagging for a pint. 'Yeah, great. Now, can we go?'

'Oh, one more thing. I'm still undecided on the floor tiles, Jess.'

'Jesus Christ! Can't you sort that out some other time?'

'Not really, darling. I'd like to get it all sorted today. We haven't got much time.'

Jess could see where this was going. She decided to try and placate him. 'I'm sure we can hang on for a few more days if you want to get going. Why don't you discuss it together and let us know directly?'

'Good idea. Let's go.' He hurried Terri out of the door.

Jess shook her head – she wouldn't let anyone dictate to her like that; if she wanted to discuss interiors, she would do it no matter what. Men! Talking of which…

Taking advantage of the empty house, she rang Giles. Still no answer and he hadn't contacted her or left a message. She wondered if she'd done anything to piss him off but couldn't think of anything. Oh, well. He was probably at his yacht club or at his boathouse. She would try again later.

*

The twins had been pestering their mother all week to go round and see Auntie Jess's new flat, so this evening Mandy had given in. Kirsty and Keira wanted to play a trick on Jess – wanting to look grown-up they asked Mandy to hide when they rang the door bell.

'Go on, then. I'll be round here,' said Mandy, pointing to the side of the building behind the bin store.

They argued over which of them was going to press the bell; in the end they both pressed it. Jess opened the door and the twins started chuckling.

'Hi ya. You haven't walked round here on your own?' said Jess, peering out.

They both gave her a toothy grin and tried not to give the game away. After a few seconds Mandy emerged. 'No, of course not, you hear some dreadful things these days.'

'Yeah, too right.'

'Can we see your new flat, Auntie Jess?' pleaded Keira.

'Course you can. Come on.'

The twins raced upstairs and started looking around. Mandy followed and told them not to go touching anything.

'They're OK. I'll give you the grand tour if you like,' said Jess, and took Mandy into the bedroom then the bathroom and finally back to the living area with the kitchenette.

Mandy smiled. 'It's lovely, Jess. I bet you're over the moon?'

'Yeah, it's cool. I was just getting some ideas for the bedroom. What do you think?' She showed Mandy a page in a *Homes* magazine with shades of grey and accents of purple.

'Yeah, nice, but don't you think it's a bit cold-looking?'

'Nope. I think it's more sophisticated.'

Mandy considered this. Jess seemed to be changing her opinions. She hadn't looked as if she was really enjoying Saucy Meg's either. 'What happened when we left the other night?'

'Not much. Danny's mate was so pissed he knocked his beer all over me. I was soaked right through to my underwear. I came straight home and jumped in the shower.'

'Seeing him again?'

'Huh, you're joking.'

The twins were bored. 'Can we have a drink, Auntie?' asked Keira.

'Course, and drop all this Auntie stuff. It makes me feel old!'

The twins grinned and followed Jess to the fridge.

'What would you like?'

'Juice please, Auntie,' Kirsty clapped her hands to her mouth, her mischievous eyes shining. Jess smiled too and poured out two tumblers of orange juice. Mandy told them to sit down with it; she didn't want them spilling any. Jess found something on the telly for them to watch and they both sat quietly.

Mandy wanted the latest. 'So, how's Giles, then?''

'You'll never guess.'

'What? He's asked you to marry him?'

Jess shook her head. 'Nah, but Cruella's divorcing him!'

'No! Well, that's a start.'

'She claims she saw us together in the summerhouse.'

'Blimey! So what's gonna happen now?'

'Dunno, but Giles is doing his best to keep her mitts off his money. She's trying to screw him to the ground, so we'll have to wait and see. I haven't seen or heard from him since yesterday morning, probably at his yacht club or down his boathouse.'

Mandy got the picture. But she wondered why Jess wanted to be bothered with a married man and one that was out of her comfort zone. 'He hasn't rung you then?'

'Nope, but you should see his apartment, Mandy, and the awesome house his parents live in.'

'Yeah, OK, but how do you feel about *him*.' Mandy still thought Jess should patch it up with Eddie. They used to be so good together, from what she remembered.

Jess took a while to answer. She still wasn't sure about Giles but she didn't want to go into details with Mandy. Not yet. 'Well, he's no Romeo but I could live with it.'

'Jess! You're awful!'

*

Giles came in to his apartment and chucked his keys on the hall table. He'd had an exhilarating day on the Thames racing a thirty foot yacht with Dickie and Ron. He felt alive; nothing else gave him that buzz.

After putting a Rachmaninov piano concerto on the Bose Wave System he went over to the cocktail cabinet, poured himself a large whisky and sat in his armchair, reliving the day's events. He closed his eyes and soaked up the music that filled the room. He smiled to himself; they made a good team – he, Ron and Dick.

If only it were that simple where women were concerned. There wasn't much progress being made with the divorce and he was still uncertain about Jessica. A state of limbo was forced upon him but he wasn't going to allow it to spoil his evening.

He poured himself another scotch and took it into the bedroom along with his copy of *Yachting World* and made himself comfortable on the bed, positioning the sumptuous cushions behind his head. He could still hear the piano concerto from the lounge and luxuriated in the music and his best malt whisky, transported to another world.

He absently ran his hand over the silk duvet. Jessica sprang to mind. He allowed himself the luxury of returning to that evening in the summerhouse. She'd surprised him, turned him on like no other woman but there was something he wasn't quite sure about. He didn't feel as if he had her full attention, as if her mind was elsewhere while they lay together. He pushed the thought away but another took its place.

Lydia. The bitch's solicitor had written to him asking for fifty percent of his estate on the grounds of adultery. It felt unreal for Giles to be on the other side of the fence, but thankfully Henry was fighting his corner. Giles was damned if his estranged wife was going to get what she wanted. If only he'd acted sooner and not got tangled up with Jessica – it would have been so much easier without this complication. He had a feeling Lydia was having him watched, too; it's the sort of sneaky thing she would do. Twice he had suspected a private detective hovering on the corner of the street near his office. It made Giles uneasy; he had already stated, for the sake of the divorce, that Jessica was only a one-night-stand. This was Henry's suggestion but he, Giles, had to go along with it and agree not to be seen with her for the time being. He just hoped it wouldn't get too messy.

*

Late on Monday morning, Henry Bishop sat at his office desk pondering Giles's plight. Henry had called him into his office earlier to go through a few things concerning the property in his name. Henry was determined to do his very best for Giles – he regarded him almost as a nephew, having known him since he was a toddler. He smiled, remembering the old days.

Henry and Jacob and their wives had often socialised at the Warren where they enjoyed all that the country club had to offer: golf, tennis, or outdoor bowls and a whirlwind of social engagements most weekends. Life was still treating them well but there was an underlying tension these days, what with the state of the economy threatening their pensions and now this business with Giles.

Henry felt sympathy for Giles; having married in haste and repenting at leisure. Giles had always seemed a bit of a loner to Henry; wandering around the grounds at the Warren instead of mixing with his own two boys. Truth be known, he felt sorry for him, sent off to boarding school at a tender age. But of course, it wasn't his place to interfere where Giles's upbringing was concerned; Jacob and Morwenna had his best interests at heart, or so they believed.

Henry's biggest problem now was to keep this divorce out of the public eye. Jacob didn't want the family name dragged through the mire, but it was looking more and more likely that they would have to pay Lydia to keep quiet; she had already hinted that she would take her story to the local paper if her demands were not met.

Lydia's solicitor had advised she was filing for divorce on the grounds of adultery, having evidence of Jessica being the co-respondent. Henry ruminated on the fact that Lydia had been separated from Giles for more than two years. However, for the marriage to come to an end amicably after a two year separation, the two parties had to agree, and in this case, Henry doubted it was possible. Lydia and Giles never saw eye to eye at the best of times. Giles had looked at their separation objectively; it was easier to give her a healthy allowance as well as the interior design business rather than deal with the arguments. And now Lydia saw Jessica as a threat and was determined this 'little tart' as she called her, was not going to get what she thought was rightfully hers.

Henry and Giles had discussed all of this at length, and together, they had come up with a plan, albeit a shaky one. Henry advised Giles to keep out of the public eye and postpone any engagements with Jessica. If Lydia found out they were still seeing each other, and her demands leaked out to the press, Giles and Henry would both get a pasting from Jacob.

As for the property, Henry was prepared to draw up a legal document that stated Lydia acquired the Greenwich apartment in a Transfer of Property order. It was roughly worth a million pounds at present and Giles wouldn't be sorry to lose it; he hated it anyway after Lydia had done her damndest to turn it into a morgue. But Henry now added a clause stating she would not be able to sell the apartment for at least a year, and a secondary clause stating she couldn't let it either. The way the economic climate was going this would make things far more difficult for her.

Other assets included Giles's boat house at Chichester and his yacht. Giles was adamant Lydia wasn't going to take those away from him. He would fight tooth and nail to hang onto his beloved Sea Witch and his boathouse and Henry had already safeguarded those.

All in all, Giles was going to come out of it OK, Henry decided. He clicked on 'business in hand' and closed the file.

*

On Monday evening, Giles came into his apartment, picked up his post and went into the lounge and poured himself a drink. Standing at the window in his favourite viewing place he tried to forget the week's workload and the impending divorce. His thoughts back-tracked to the last time Jessica had stood there with him. He longed to see her but after the settlement had been drawn up, the only thing he could do was talk to her on the phone.

She picked up straight away.

'Jessica, I tried to phone you on Saturday night.'

'Oh, yeah, sorry about that, I was out with me mates. You OK?'

The sound of her voice gave him an unexpected tingle of excitement. He felt a warm glow and for once it wasn't from the single malt.

'I'm well, thanks. Listen,' he went on in hushed tones, as if expecting the phone to be tapped, which he wouldn't put past Lydia. 'I'd like to see you but I've got be on my guard. I think Lydia's having me watched. I've already stated that you were only a one-night-stand so I've got to be careful.'

'Oh, thanks!'

'Sorry, you mean more to me than a one-night-stand, you know that. It's just… there's a lot at stake here.'

Jess thought about this and came up with an answer that seemed perfectly feasible to her. 'Well, can't I come to your office? No one will know I'm not a client, will they?'

He let himself be swayed. 'Yes. I suppose that could work. When's your day off?'

'Wednesday.'

Dammit. Not until then? He looked in his diary. 'What time could you get here? I think I've got a slot around four.'

'Four it is then.'

*

On Tuesday evening Jess drove round to her old flat to pick up her post. As she parked her car she noticed the For Sale board outside. So Rose was serious about moving. She turned up her nose at the shabby street with the filthy overflowing wheelie bins left haphazardly on the pavement and was thankful she was out of there.

She rang the bell. Rose came to the door in her usual purple track suit with the stains and dog's hairs.

'What do you want?'

'Hi, Rose, I've come for me post. You all right?'

'Not bad. Can't wait to move, feels very lonely now you've gone,' she said sulkily.

'Yeah, I bet,' said Jess, looking around.

Jess went to step over the threshold but Rose closed the door on her, leaving her standing on the doorstep like a door-to-door salesperson. She stood with her back to the door keeping an eye on her treasured car in case some thug decided to vandalise it. There were a few unsavoury-looking characters hovering at the end of the street. She couldn't believe how uncomfortable she felt – in the short time she had lived in Nunton it really hit her how dreadful her old living conditions had been.

After a few seconds Rose came back with Jess's mail and shoved the letters in her hand. 'Here. There's one from Australia, looks like. Nothing much apart from that.'

Jess turned her back to Rose who craned her neck to see who the blue airmail letter was from. Jess took two steps away from the door.

Her face glowed – it had been ages since she'd heard from Shelley.

'G'day, mate, from the Land Down Under!'

Jess,

I lost your email address, long story short, my old computer died, hence this letter. I hope you're sitting down when you read it. For once in our lives it's good news!

I've been doing a spot of family history and I've come up with a will. It seems our great granddad on Mum's side was a wealthy bloke! He had a chain of grocery stores in Yorkshire before the war and when he died he left some money in a trust for his son James (our granddad) for when he turned 21. Unfortunately, he died in the war before that. The inheritance should have passed to his next of kin – our dear Nan – but no one ever told her. It's all a bit of a mystery. She lost touch with James's family, so the inheritance was forgotten.

It's accrued a lot of interest over the years. Since there's no one else, wait for it – it's passed down to us. We roughly get a million each!

I've been talking to a solicitor mate of mine and he reckons you should get someone your end to check it out.

So what do you reckon? It would be great to hear from you. Such a turn-up for the books, eh?

Lots of love,

Shelley. xxx

Jess stuffed the letter back in its envelope and waved it front of Rose's nose. 'Good news for a change!'

Jess couldn't wait to get home and phone Shelley. She thought of all the things she was going to do with her newly found wealth – new car, buy her own house, shop in Harrods, the list was endless. It was going to be fab. And she had a landline now, too, after Mandy had advised her it would be a good idea and lent her the money.

She let herself in, kicked off her shoes and put the kettle on. She took her address book out of the drawer and found Shelley's number.

'Hell, mate! It's four thirty in the morning! Who's this?'

'Shelley? It's me, Jess! Just got your letter. Sorry. Do you want me to ring back later? I forgot the time difference.'

'Jess! Yeah, er… no. Oh, mate, it's great to hear from you! How you doing?'

'Yeah, I'm good. Even better after the news. Wow, I can't believe it!'

'What news?'

'The will?'

'Oh, yeah that,' Shelley was beginning to come round. 'Yeah, I know. I couldn't believe it either. Geez, I've got such a lot to tell you. You OK to talk?'

Jess threw caution to the wind. She would face the extortionate phone bill when it came in. 'Yeah, go ahead.'

'Christ! I don't know where to start. Well, I told you most of it in the letter, didn't I? But wait, what you won't know is that our great-great-grandmother had an affair with an artist called Edward Clarke. The result of this was our great- grandfather, Walter; he's the one who had the string of grocer's shops in Yorkshire.'

'Blimey!'

'Yeah, I know. I've got the paperwork here, somewhere.' Jess heard her sister rummaging around. 'Right. He was illegitimate. His mother married John Nelson, so Walter took his name. Walter married Mary and they had James who died in the war when he was nineteen. James – this all gets a bit complicated – married a lady in London called Phoebe, that's our Nan. She was pregnant with our mum when James got killed and she was left penniless. She lost touch with his family and the rest is history, as they say.'

'God! It's like something out of a film, init?'

'Ha! Yeah.'

'Hang on, you sure this is right? I didn't know Nan's name was Phoebe.'

'Oh yeah, she didn't use it, didn't like it, but that was her name all right.'

Jess's mind was running on ahead. 'An artist, you said?'

'Yeah, that's right. Edward Clarke. I think he painted landscapes or something. Don't know if he was famous though.'

Jess went quiet. Her thoughts sprang to the painting in Giles's apartment. 'What sort of landscapes?'

'Geez, I dunno, probably Yorkshire ones. Why?'

'Wasn't there a rumour about a painting in the family that got lost?'

'Oh yeah, that's right. Anyway, my lawyer mate, Jason has looked into it but you need to get someone to go through it with you, Jess.'

'How much do you reckon we're worth, then?' Jess's heart was banging against her ribs.

'Well, this is the great bit. Walter, bless him, put some of his property into a trust for James, I think it was in 1940. It means we get roughly just over a million… each!'

'That's what I thought you said in your letter. But it can't be, surely?'

'Nope, it's the truth mate, according to Jason. He's done all the calculations.'

'Blimey, I can't believe this.'

'But like I said, you'll have to get a lawyer your end to follow it up.'

'Something else I've gotta tell you – I've met a lawyer called Giles Morgan; I've been seeing him since the end of April. He should be able to help me with this.'

'Great! Even better. What's he like?'

'Cool, loaded, but his estranged wife is a bitch. She suspects us of having an affair and she's onto him.'

'Geez! You never did things by halves, kid!'

Jess giggled. It really was quite bizarre when she thought about it. 'It's so good to hear from you, Shel, but I'd better go. I don't know how much this call is costing me… but hey! I don't have to worry now, though, do I?'

'No, that's right. To think of poor Mum and Dad and Nan how they struggled. I wonder what they'd say?'

'Maybe they're all looking down on us right now. Who knows?'

'Yeah, what a thought, eh?'

'Yeah, speak soon. Bye, Shel.'

This really was too good to be true. And Edward Clarke. Cool.

Oh my God. What to do first? She was bursting to tell Mandy and she would have to see Giles and check out the painting for a signature. She rang Mandy but used her mobile – she didn't want to rack up too much of a bill just in case it transpired that the will was false.

'Hi, Jess. You OK?'

'Yeah thanks, I've just rung Shelley in Australia.'

'Blimey! Not on your mobile?'

'No, I used the landline. Thanks for doing that for me. Anyway, listen, you'll never guess – I went round the old flat to get me post and I had a letter from Shelley telling me, wait for it... are you sitting down?'

'Yeah, why?'

'Oh my God, Mandy, we've come into money. I can't believe it. She's been doing some research and our great-grandfather left some money in a trust for his son, but he got killed in the war and the will was forgotten. So now it passes down to Shelley and me.'

'I'm coming round!'

A little while later Jess ran down to open the door to Mandy who flung her arms round her. 'Wow, Jess! How fantastic.'

'I know, come up. I've got the kettle on.'

'We should be drinking champagne, I dunno about tea.'

Too excited to sit down, the two of them went over the letter together and talked about what this meant for Jess.

'How much, if you don't mind me asking?'

Jess beamed. 'Well at the moment, it looks like a million!'

'Wow! Five hundred K each.'

'No, a million. Each!'

Mandy fell onto the sofa. 'You're joking?'

'Nope. I'm seeing Giles tomorrow afternoon. I'll ask him to check it out.'

'Lucky you met him. What do you think he'll say?'

'I dunno.' She suddenly went quiet. 'Mandy? You won't tell anyone, will you? Not till I know for sure?'

'No, course not. Cross my heart and hope to die,' she said, crossing herself. 'Not even Trev.'

CHAPTER FIFTEEN

Jess came out of Razor Sharp feeling like a new woman. She'd asked Mark to do a pink 'balayage' on her hair – a subtle graduation from blonde at the roots to bright pink on the ends. It had been an odd experience to say the least – she'd never had her hair done anywhere but Top to Toe – and Mark, with a shaved head, tattoos and earrings, was nothing like she'd imagined Chris's son. She wasn't used to paying to have her hair done either, but hey, what did it matter now as long as the will was legit?

She glanced at her watch. God! Where had the time gone? Giles was expecting her at four o'clock and it was now four thirty. She drove like the wind hoping she'd be able to find a parking space and that he hadn't gone home.

She cheekily managed to find a space in the staff car park at the back of the building and rushed into Morgan Bishop, slightly out of breath. The Mouse glanced up from her desk. 'Can I help you?'

'Yes. Jessica Harvey. I have an appointment with Mr Morgan at four o'clock. Sorry I'm late.'

Gloria peered at Jess over her glasses and spoke into the intercom. 'Jessica Harvey's in reception, Mr Morgan.'

Jess heard the reply, 'Show her in, would you?'

Jess bypassed the Mouse and entered Giles's office. He locked the door behind them and pulled her to him. 'I thought you weren't coming. God! I've missed you!'

Jess peeled herself away and smiled at him. 'Sorry I'm late. Mark took longer than I thought.'

'Mark?' he scowled.

'Yeah, he owns Razor Sharp.'

Giles looked blank.

'The hairdresser's?'

Giles stood back and studied her more carefully then it dawned on him. 'Good God, what the hell have you done to your hair?'

Jess was on the defensive straight away. 'Huh, well, I think it's cool.'

'I don't. It makes you look cheap.'

She turned away and slumped in the easy chair. 'I can do what I want.'

'Yes, you can, but not with me!' He walked back behind his desk and looked out the window.

She was tempted to leave and come back when he was in a better mood, but she was desperate for his opinion on the will.

'Anyway, I'm here in a professional capacity,' she said, getting up and handing him the letter.

'What's this?'

'It's from my sister. She's been doing a spot of family history.'

Giles opened it and started to read, intermittently looking up at Jess and walking around his office. Finally, he pulled up a chair and sat down in front of her. He wasn't sure what to make of this; it could go one of two ways for him. If it was true, and she had come into money, she might feel more his equal. On the other hand, he might not see her for dust.

Jess was impatient. 'Well? What d'you think?'

'Mm, I don't know. If it's true...'

'Course it's true! Shelley wouldn't tell me otherwise.'

'Yes, but these things can be very complicated. I'll have to look into it.'

'I know that. That's what I'm asking you. How long will it take?'

Giles decided it could be to his advantage to stall for time. 'It's difficult to say. It all depends on how much is involved.'

'Now you're sounding like a lawyer.'

'Look, I'll do my best. In all probability you could come out of this a rich woman.'

'I know that. I just thought you'd be more helpful.' She stood up.

Thinking she was about to leave, he shot out of his chair and held her by her arms. 'Jessica, I know how much this means to you but I don't want you to get your hopes up.'

She shrugged him off. She had half a mind to find another lawyer, one without any interest in her personal life.

'OK. Leave it with me. I'll check it out.' He went to kiss her again but she turned her head away. 'I'm sorry. Your hair was a bit of a shock, that's all. Maybe it'll grow on me.'

As always, she turned it into a joke. 'It'd look funny on you!'

Giles smiled, relieved. 'Am I forgiven?' Good God, what was he thinking? He'd never in all his born days asked a woman to forgive him, but the words tumbled out before he could stop them.

She nodded but decided to withhold her affections until he had looked into the legacy. She stared into his eyes. 'How's the divorce going?'

He sighed. She certainly knew how to dampen his ardour. 'I'm afraid Lydia's being very difficult. She's threatened to take her story to the papers if she doesn't get what she wants.'

'And what does she want?'

'Too much.'

'So, what happens now?'

'Well, the petition has gone to court but it looks likely I'll have to give her a huge amount to shut her up.'

'But that's blackmail!'

'Precisely, but I can't see a way round it without it costing me a lot of money. Either way, she thinks she's got the upper hand. It's a bloody mess but Henry's doing his damndest. The fact is she deserted me over two years ago, so it could work in my favour.'

Jess shrugged. 'So?'

'It's a tricky one. It could take months, years, if she won't agree. Not to mention the cost.' He went over to the window and looked up and down the road.

'What are you doing?'

'I think Lydia's having me watched, I told you. Did you notice anyone lurking on the corner?'

'God, no! I was late, remember?'

'Yes, of course. I'm sorry,' he came towards her. 'Come here.' His eyes were dark with desire. 'Jessica, I want us to be together.'

He pulled her to him, pressed his lips on hers, grazing her teeth. 'Come with me to the boathouse this weekend.'

'But what about the detective?'

'To hell with it! She'll do what she wants, anyway.'

'But I'm cooking lunch for Mandy and Trevor on Sunday.'

'That's OK. We can leave here early Friday evening and be back on Saturday night.'

Anything to please, he was desperate. With a bit of luck, she wouldn't want to come back on Saturday. He wanted her. Nothing else mattered. Her perfume was sending shock waves through him. 'Come upstairs,' he breathed, 'I've got a private room up there. No one will bother us. Please, Jessica.'

She shook her head and strode towards the door. 'See you later.'

*

Giles picked up the phone on Thursday evening.

'Hi. I need to see you.'

This was more like it. She *needed* him. 'OK, do you want to come here, to the apartment?'

'Yeah. I'll be round in two shakes.'

Giles rubbed his hands together. A bottle of Pinot Grigio on ice, soft music on the Bose Wave system...

Jess drove as fast as the traffic would allow, managed to park her car in the last space outside his apartment and walked up to the intercom.

'Hi, it's me.'

'Come on up.'

Giles went to greet her with a kiss but she pushed past him to examine the painting over the fireplace.

He was dumbstruck. 'What are you doing?'

She stood looking at the picture of Coverdale – the stream, the trees and the countryside; it was all there but difficult to define. As before, she could just detect a reclining figure under the trees in the foreground. It was hard to see at first, it was so dark. Her eyes scanned the edges of the painting. Yes! There was a signature on the right-hand side. She could just make it out.

'Oh my God, it's true!'

'What is?'

'The painting.'

'What about it?'

'Long story.'

'What, another one?'

'No, the same one, really.'

'Look, Jessica, what's this is all about?'

She couldn't take her eyes off the landscape. She could imagine Edward painting the picture of her great-great-grandmother asleep under the tree. 'OK, look – my great- great-grandmother – I don't know her name – had an affair with the artist who painted this picture – Edward Clarke. That's his signature. See?' she said pointing. 'They had an illegitimate son, Walter, my great-grandfather.'

'But that's ridiculous! How on earth has this got anything to do with you? It's Lydia's painting.'

'I don't know. It's weird. What do you know about her family history?'

'Not much, except that she comes from a very respectable family in Yorkshire.'

Jess went cold. Surely she wasn't related to Cruella? 'I need a drink.'

'But you're driving.'

'I don't care. I'll get a taxi or something.'

'Jessica. What is it?'

'If my suspicions are right, I'm related to Lydia.'

'Good God!' Giles went over to the cocktail cabinet, poured two whiskies and handed one to Jess. They both sat down on the sofa, staring at the painting.

'I'm going to have to do a bit of research of my own,' said Jess, 'Shelley told me about this artist but she doesn't know anything about Lydia. Have you looked into the will?'

'No, not yet. I haven't had time.' Giles didn't like the sound of this one bit. If Jessica was related to his wife, was there some similarity he wasn't aware of? Did he even want to pursue the relationship? He wanted to inspect the will for an entirely different reason now – his own piece of mind.

'I'll start tomorrow. It's even more important now.'

'Oh, yeah? Who for?'

'Well, for all concerned, really.'

'I don't believe this. I just want you to find out if this will is legit and what I'm entitled to, otherwise I'll get another lawyer onto it, one who's got no interest in my personal life!'

He grabbed her hand and pulled her towards him. 'Come here. Don't get upset. Have you eaten? Do you want to go out for something?'

She snatched her hand away and got up to leave. 'Nah, I've lost me appetite. I'll see you later.'

'What about the weekend?'

'Stuff the weekend and your bloody boathouse!'

She rushed out of the apartment and banged the door.

He winced. She'd left a token of lipstick on the glass he'd just given her. He picked it up and ran his thumb over it, setting his juices flowing, but his desire for her turned to anger. Now he knew what it was he couldn't put his finger on; the rumour must be true and both women were now holding him to ransom – Lydia for his money, Jessica for his affections. A few weeks ago the only problems he had were work-related. Now he felt split in two. Damn the opposite sex! The only woman that didn't give him grief was Sea Witch. He would go on his own at the weekend and to hell with it.

*

Jess came in on Saturday evening, kicked off her shoes, put the kettle on and popped a pizza in the oven. Taking the documents out of her bag she sat down and started to go through them. She'd been to The Family Record Centre all afternoon looking into the records of the other side of the family – Lydia's side. Luckily, the staff had been very helpful. Studying the censuses, birth, death and marriage certificates was fascinating and addictive and the time flew.

From the census she had found out that her great-grandfather, Walter, was married to Mary. There were two children, a boy James, and a girl Jean. James was Jess's grandfather who died in the war. From the other records she'd found out James's sister Jean, had married Jack Hamilton. Jean and Jack had a son, Charles, who married Louisa and they had a daughter – Lydia.

So here was the evidence – Lydia was Jess and Shelley's cousin. She also found out that Lydia was a twin, but the other one had died a few days after the birth. Bloody hell! Imagine two like her. She thought of telling Eddie, the two of them laughing together and she wondered whether to tell him about the will. She could imagine him picking her up and swinging her round, taking her out to celebrate...

But she was getting carried away, she told herself to focus on the records again. There were also some trades directories and she promised herself another day to go back and read up on those. If what Shelley had told her was true, Walter had been a big noise in the food industry in Leeds before the war. It seemed highly likely that his daughter Jean and son-in-law Jack would have inherited the grocery business. Thank God good old Walter had put the rest in a trust.

Jess sat with her cup of tea wondering what those days must have been like for her great-grandparents, Walter and Mary. She studied the printout of the 1911 census again: their address was Roundhay Park, Leeds. She looked at it in more detail. Oh my God! They also had a housemaid and a cook. The other houses on the census sheet were of similar size, all with interesting inhabitants; important people such as bankers and lawyers. She found it hard to believe that she knew nothing of this part of the family until a few days ago. What had happened that her side of the family had been reduced to such poverty? She would have to go back when she had more time and find out. Shelley had said that James married Phoebe, their Nan from London. How had that come about when he was from Yorkshire? And why didn't Phoebe know anything about his family?

She drained her cup. So Lydia was her cousin. This was hard to digest. Jess was frightened that Lydia would get wind of this legacy and get her hands on the money that was rightfully hers and Shelley's. Hopefully, Giles would do his homework and it wouldn't come to that.

After settling down on the sofa with her much needed pizza, Jess checked the time and rang Shelley – it was early on Sunday morning in Sydney.

'Hi, Jess. Hang on – I'll just get my breakfast.'

Jess waited impatiently for Shelley to come back. She heard some clattering about in the background and then Shelley munching.

'OK. Fire away.'

'I've just been to The Family History centre. Do you wanna know what I've found out?'

'Yeah, go on.'

Shelley listened while she ate her breakfast; she was fascinated with what Jess had to tell her and after a lengthy conversation, Shelley filled in a few of the gaps.

Phoebe and James had had a whirlwind romance and like so many couples after the war, they didn't want to waste time on an engagement. After a few weeks, they'd been married by special license in a London register office while he'd been home on leave. He'd never told her much about his parents except they were well-heeled. The age-old problem of the class divide meant she would never meet them and when James was killed, Phoebe was on her own and pregnant. She had no family of her own to call on for support. Her baby Lily was born in a London nursing home and she had to make the best of things which was very difficult after the war. The social services were only able to help up to a point – she was just one among the many people who had been made homeless after the blitz. Life had been a struggle but she brought Lily up to be well-mannered and thoughtful and impressed on her how important it was to keep body and soul together. 'Waste not, want not' was a favourite saying.

Lily, Jess and Shelley's mum, married Fred Harvey in 1970. Phoebe was disappointed: wanting her daughter to have a better life than the one she'd had. She thought Lily could have done a lot better for herself, but Lily wouldn't have anything said against Fred and fell out with her mother. Fred Harvey came from a long line of dockers and stevedores but he fell on hard times when the last of the docks closed. He found a job in the canning factory but life was difficult for them. Shelley was born in 1976 and Jessica in 1989, but being an older mum Lily died after she gave birth to Jess and Phoebe stepped in to help Fred bring up his daughters.

'How do you think Phoebe met James, then?' asked Jess.

'I think James palled up with some bloke from London who was fighting with him in the war. They came home on leave together and James met this man's family and stayed with them, that's when he met her. I think there was talk of James settling in London after the war and the father helping him to get a job.'

'Yeah, sounds possible. I don't suppose we'll ever really know?'

'Nope. There's only a certain amount you can find out from records. The rest you have to fill in, like a detective.'

'Talking of which, that brings me back to Cruella.'

'Who?'

'Oh, it's my nickname for Lydia.' Jess heard Shelley snigger on the other end. 'She's having Giles watched by a private detective.'

'Hell, mate! What have you gotten yourself into? I'd steer clear if I was you.'

'Yeah, but he's helping me with the will, or says he is.'

'Listen, if he's dragging his feet get another lawyer onto it. He sounds a bit of a bludger.'

'Don't worry, I'm onto it. Oh, it's so good to talk to you, Shel. I wish you were here.'

'Yeah, I've been thinking – Jason reckons I'll need to come over and sign some documents; I could get a flight for your birthday.'

'Wow! You'd have to share my bed, though.'

'Don't worry about me; I'll shack up at the local youth hostel.'

'You don't wanna do that. You could stay with Mandy; that'd be cool. I'll ask her tomorrow.'

'Well, we're not exactly short of cash now, are we? If the worst comes to the worst, I could always stay at the Savoy!'

*

Giles sat cradling a glass of single malt and watching the rain bouncing off the harbour wall. The evening was prematurely drawing in, putting him in an even blacker mood. He had hoped for an exhilarating day's sailing to take his mind off his problems but that had proved impossible. Sea Witch had handled well as always but there was little or no wind which forced him to resort to engine power, which he was loath to do, and he had decided to call it a day.

His thoughts turned to his grandfather; he had decided to pay him a visit before coming down to the boathouse. Sam was delighted Giles had called on him and all ears about the events leading up to the weekend. He listened intently as Giles told him about the likelihood of the connection between Lydia and Jessica and about the will.

Sam had asked him, 'How do you feel about Jessica, now? She's causing quite a stir in your life, isn't she?'

Giles sat looking down at his hands and took a while to answer. Finally he looked at Sam and said, 'I think I'm in love with her…'

'…But?'

A weak smile played around Giles's mouth. 'You know me too well.' He tried not to sound pathetic. 'There's a nagging doubt at the back of my mind.'

'That's only to be expected. You haven't had the best of experiences with women. My advice is to stay away for a while and see how you feel then, absence makes the heart grow fonder, to quote an old saying, especially if you think Lydia's having you watched.'

'Yes but the trouble is it looks like Lydia and Jessica may have the same tendencies, similarities that may come out later on.'

'Surely not, Jessica's had a totally different upbringing.'

'Yes, but her sister has looked into the family history. I can't help thinking there's something in the genes, I don't know, something deep-seated.'

'In what way?'

'I'm not sure but it turns out Jessica and Lydia are cousins and you know what happened to her great-grandmother.'

'Really? So what you're saying is – you think Jessica has the same... instability?'

Giles nodded.

'To be fair, it's early days. How long have you known her?'

'Nearly five weeks.'

Sam smiled to himself at the quick retort. 'Like I said, give it time. Has there been anything to suggest a mental health issue where Jessica is concerned?'

Giles thought about the last time he saw Jessica. He flinched inwardly. 'It's just that she lost her temper and banged the door the last time she came to see me.'

Sam smiled. 'Women who fly off the handle can be very passionate in bed, you know.'

Giles felt a little awkward to hear his grandfather talking openly about sex. He hoped he wasn't going to get a lecture. He thought it a little late in the day for that sort of thing.

'What's the matter? Didn't you think an old dog like me would still think about sex?'

Giles smiled and shook his head.

Sam chuckled but he could tell there was something Giles wasn't telling him. He was still very pensive. 'What else is troubling you? Is it the money?'

Giles sighed, walked over to the window and stood looking out. 'Yes... No... Oh, I don't know. I think Henry's got it pretty much sewn up but I know I've got a fight on my hands with Lydia.'

'I think you'll be all right. But as I said before Giles, only you can weigh it up. Let me know how you get on.'

CHAPTER SIXTEEN

The Mouse spoke into the intercom. 'Your father is on the phone, Mr Morgan.'

'Thank you, Gloria. Put him through, would you?'

Jacob was less than happy; he'd just read the local paper. Giles and Lydia's divorce was front page news.

'What?' Giles shouted down the phone. 'But we stated in the divorce settlement that Lydia would get a lump sum if she kept her mouth shut.'

'Do you mean to tell me you knew about this all along? Good God, man. She'll ruin us!'

'Not if Henry gets his way.'

'Well, that's as maybe. I don't like the sound of this one iota. I think the best thing you can do is to lay low for a while, go to your boathouse or something. How the hell has it come to this?'

Giles didn't have any answers. He felt a spike of heat as he had as a child standing before his father while he reprimanded him.

'Well, Giles, you're on your own with this one; you're not dragging us down with you. I'm a respected pillar of the community, for God's sake. How the hell do you think this'll go down at The Lodge and the Warren?'

'Well, I think you're blowing this up out of all proportion, to be fair...'

'I don't! What on earth were you thinking, for Christ's sake?'

Giles wondered how to placate his father but there was a slight glimmer of hope. 'It's not all bad. It turns out that Jessica has come into a small fortune and – wait for it – she's related to Lydia in a roundabout way.'

'What? You mean that blond bit is part of Lydia's family?'

'Yes, cousins and she's not a blond bit!'

'Oh, all right. And the fortune?'

'Long story – something to do with the painting over the fireplace in the Greenwich apartment.'

'You mean it's worth a lot of money?'

'I don't know. No, not exactly. Lydia and Jessica share the same great-great- grandfather; he's the one who painted the picture. And their great-grandfather left the legacy.'

Jacob mulled this over for a few seconds. If Jessica was part of Lydia's family, would Lydia know about the history behind the painting? And if she did, surely she would want to protect it, make sure the blonde tart didn't get her hands on it. 'Does Lydia know about this, about the two of them sharing the same great-grandparents?'

'Not as far as I know, and I don't plan on telling her, either.'

Jacob was becoming intrigued by this story. It might not be so bad if Jessica had links with Lydia's highly regarded family. 'Has Jessica asked you to look into the will?'

'Yes. Her great-grandfather left a substantial amount of money in a trust for his son who died in the Second World War before he could claim it. It passed to his next of kin, of course. Long story short, it's passed down to Jessica and her sister.'

'I see. She's got a sister?'

'Yes, in Australia. She's the one who looked into the family history and discovered the will.'

'All right but I still advise you get away for a while. I don't want the media pouncing on any more of this story. God only knows what Lydia's parents will think of all this.'

'But what about my work? I'm snowed under this week.'

'I'll come up and look after things if you've got no one else to step in. It'll give me a chance to catch up with Henry. Ha! It'll be like old times!'

Giles was relieved at the outcome of their conversation, but, nevertheless, he had been well and truly put in his place. Dammit. He couldn't get over the fact that Lydia had reneged on their deal, but then again, he should have realised and seen this coming. Damn the woman. Damn her to hell!

He suddenly had the idea that it would be an ideal opportunity to go to Yorkshire and do a spot of research on Jessica's behalf and also put his own mind at rest. He could look into the will at the registry and find out a few more details about Jessica's family history.

He spoke into the intercom and asked Gloria to make an open ended reservation at the Park Hotel in Harrogate commencing tomorrow evening. The Mouse had seen the local paper and had tried to listen in to Giles's conversation with his father, but having other calls to attend to, she hadn't managed to glean much from it. She came into his office and sidled up to him, hoping to be let in on the gossip. 'Going away, Mr Morgan?'

'Yes. I've got some business to attend to in Yorkshire. You'll be working with my father over the coming week.'

Gloria's face lit up. 'Oh, that'll make a nice change,' her hand flew to her mouth. 'Sorry, I didn't mean...'

He let out a sigh. 'That'll be all, Gloria.'

She scurried off.

When he arrived home, Giles told Joan of his plans and that his father would be staying the week, in his place. She was intrigued and more than happy to be of service to her former employer. 'My goodness! I haven't seen Mr Jacob for ages. It'll be like old times.'

'Yes,' was all Giles could manage. It was pretty obvious that Jacob's staff had held him in high regard, what with The Mouse's reaction and now Joan's, but there was only one woman Giles wanted to impress right now and his trip to Yorkshire might just win her round.

*

Jess was driving back to the office of Jenkins & Co. after a busy day, thinking about the Sunday lunch she had cooked for Mandy, Trevor and the twins the day before. The roast chicken and all the trimmings had been a great success, everyone had enjoyed it even Kirsty and Keira who were usually finicky eaters. Jess had never been allowed to be fussy; she'd told them what her father used to say when she didn't want her dinner and the twins giggled, so did Mandy and Trevor. It was good to be in their company, the closest thing she'd had to a family for years. When Jess told them about Shelley coming over for her birthday Mandy was only too pleased to put her up and the twins were ecstatic at the thought of having Auntie Jess's sister to stay.

Jess had been thinking more about Mandy and Trevor recently. Every time she was in their company she got the impression they were the epitome of a devoted couple with a happy home life. She couldn't picture Giles in that set-up – life with him would be one long round of social engagements and dinner parties. She doubted children would ever come into the equation.

While she was parking her car she noticed a photographer taking pictures outside the office. He watched Jess enter Jenkins & Co, pointed his camera at her and clicked. Cool. She wondered if Chris had contacted the local paper to promote the business and went in to find him. But first, she checked her phone for messages. There was one from Giles.

'Jessica, I'm going away for a few days to check out the will. Try not to worry about the local news reports. I'll let you know how I get on. Speak to you soon.'

News reports? What was he talking about? She listened to the message again and went over to Chris's desk to find the local paper. Sure enough, there was a picture of her with Giles coming out of the Terrace Restaurant and a story about his divorce. So there *had* been someone watching them, and she thought Giles was just being paranoid.

Wait a minute, she was a celebrity! Cool, as long as the subject of the will didn't leak out. But she hadn't told anyone apart from Mandy and Trevor so she should be safe on that score.

Chris walked in. 'Ah, Jess, I've been meaning to have a word. Step into the staff room, would you?' He closed the door behind them. 'Jess… no doubt you're aware your picture's in the paper?'

Jess nodded. 'Yeah, cool eh?'

'Yes…' he rubbed a hand over his beard, 'but I'm a bit concerned. I think it might be a good idea to take some time off. Things might get a bit awkward.'

'Oh, there's no need, I'm fine with it, really. And the publicity might help your business.'

He smiled at her reaction. 'Well, yes, there is that, of course. But to be forewarned is to be forearmed, OK?'

'Yeah, sure.'

'Well, if you've finished here, maybe you'd like to get away early?'

'Oh. OK.'

She was a bit puzzled but thought she ought to do as he suggested. Surely his reaction was a bit over-the-top? As she collected her things, Cynthia and Janet glanced up at her but they said nothing.

Back at her apartment, her mobile was ringing as she entered the front door. She answered it as she ran upstairs. Mandy wanted to know if she'd seen her picture in the paper.

'Yeah, I know. Cool, eh?'

'You're famous, Jess! Everyone's talking about you at work. How does Giles feel about it?'

'I don't know but he left a message on me phone saying he's gone away for a few days to check out the will. Oh, Mandy! I can't wait to hold that document in my hands.'

Mandy, ever cautious, hoped Jess wasn't going to be disappointed after all this but showed her excitement all the same. 'Yeah, I'd love to see your face when you get it!'

'You never know, you might be needed as a witness.'

'Fantastic!' Mandy was feeling almost as excited as Jess. 'Do you fancy meeting up with Connie and Sarah tomorrow evening at The Place? They're itching to get in on the goss.'

'As long as they don't know anything about the will. I'll be gutted if it gets out.'

'Well, if they do, they haven't heard it from me.'

'OK. I'll meet you down there about seven.'

As soon as Jess put the phone down it rang again; this time it was Eddie. He'd also seen the paper.

'Christ, Jess! You wanna be careful; you could get yourself in a lot of trouble.'

'Why? I'm fine with it. I'm a celeb Eddie! How cool is that? There's a crowd of us meeting up at The Place tomorrow night. Look, why don't you join us?'

'No thanks, love. Not really my scene.'

There was an awkward pause; he really wanted to see her on her own and fell back on the only reason he could think of. 'Car going OK? I was thinking… I ought to come round and check your tyres one evening.'

She absently told him to pop round on Thursday; she wasn't doing anything.

Jess was just putting the kettle on when the phone rang again. Becky wanted to catch up on the latest too, seeing as she had been there on that fateful night, so Jess asked her to meet them all tomorrow night.

*

On Wednesday morning Jess arrived at work looking worse for wear. She went straight to the coffee machine and poured herself a strong black one.

As soon as she had stepped inside The Place last night, all her friends whistled and cheered at the sight of her disguise in a black wig and dark glasses. The cocktails had flowed all night and everyone was caught up in the whirlwind of excitement. They all wanted to know what Giles was like, why he wasn't with her, what she was going to do now and had he asked to her marry him and Becky told her she would do the catering for her wedding. Danny had heard on the grapevine that Jess was going to put in an appearance. Hoping for some of the publicity to rub off on him, he never left her side all evening. He kept asking her to join his am-dram group but she still declined and the whole thing got out of hand with Sarah hoping Danny would take notice of her instead. Mandy was the only one who could stand back and look at it objectively. She thought Jess might come a cropper, especially if the will was a hoax and decided she would be there for her when it happened. But Jess had enjoyed being the centre of attention until she had gone home feeling a bit worse for wear.

This morning, Chris took one look at her and decided she should lay low for a while. There were more photos, this time on social media, of Jess coming out of The Place with Danny.

'Take a week off, Jess. You never know when or where the paparazzi will strike next. It's all very well at first, a novelty, but it soon starts to wear a bit thin.'

Jess scrolled through the photos on Chris's laptop. 'Well I need to do something. If Giles sees this he'll have a meltdown.'

Chris nodded. 'Like I said, take a week off. I'll be able to handle things here.'

'Thanks, Chris.'

He smiled. At least she was seeing sense. 'Keep in touch and let me know how you get on.'

Jess thought this was wise. After all, the more publicity, the more likelihood there was of the will leaking out. She could imagine Lydia rubbing her hands together; the bitch must be revelling in all this.

In his hotel room, Giles looked at his phone and noticed the same photos of Jess coming out of The Place with Danny. What the devil was she playing at? He had to get her out of London; if Jacob saw this there would be hell to pay. Also his jealousy had reared up at the sight of her with someone else. He decided to ask her to join him in Harrogate. He rang her number. It went straight to voicemail. Not wanting to leave a message he decided to ring again later this evening.

Meanwhile, there was some more research to be getting on with regarding Jess's great-grandfather Walter and his estate. Giles had already been to the York Probate Registry and after a long search, had found that there was indeed a will, or rather a property trust that Walter had left to his son James in 1938. Giles wanted to find out why. The more he dug into the records the more curious he became. He would to go back to Castle Chambers and search the records for former employees of local businesses and also look at the old newspapers for clues.

*

To make the most of her time off Jess went home and decided to give her apartment a thorough clean. She pulled out the sofa to vacuum behind it and came across a little notebook and pencil belonging to the twins. She placed it on the coffee table and resolved to take it round later.

After doing some more jobs she made a cup of coffee and curled up on the sofa. Her eyes fell upon the little notebook; it intrigued her. She knew she shouldn't – it was private – but her fingers itched to turn the pages. To her surprise it was written in the form of a diary with little drawings of Jess with yellow hair and their mother with purple and the words: 'Mummy and Aunty Jess are frenz. We luv Aunty Jess.'

Another page said 'Aunty Jess is very pritty. Mummy sez she needs a nice boyfrend but not Jyls. Eddy luvs her.'

So, this is what Mandy thought, was it? She would have to have it out with her next time they met up.

As if on cue Jess's phone rang.

'Jessica. It's Giles. How are you?'

'Not bad. Chris has given me the rest of the week off – he's worried about the photos in the media.'

'Perfect. How would you like to come up and join me in Yorkshire? It would be an ideal opportunity to have a few days away, just the two of us.'

'Wow! I'd love to. I've never been to Yorkshire and I could find out a bit more about me great-granddad, too.'

'Yes. You'll be glad to know I've been to the registry and done the boring bits.'

'Wicked! So what have you found out?'

'I'll tell you when I see you. I don't want you driving all that way, though. I've looked up the times of the trains and one comes into Harrogate tomorrow about three. I'll meet you at the station.'

*

At ten to three on Thursday afternoon, Jess felt a tingle of apprehension as the train slowed and pulled into Harrogate. Never having been far from home she didn't know what to expect but she was looking forward to staying in a plush hotel. And knowing Giles, it would be one of the best.

The train journey had been an eye-opener – the last time she'd been on one she'd been very young and the trains were very different. She couldn't remember much about it, or where she went but the distant memory showed her going somewhere with her Nan. It was all very hazy.

Stepping off the train she spotted Giles walking towards her, smiling. He was casually dressed and looked very relaxed. He greeted her with a brief kiss on the lips. 'Jessica. Good journey?'

'Yeah, thanks. Blimey, Kings Cross was busy, never seen so many people in one place.'

'Here, let me take your case.'

Jess couldn't stop talking about all the gossip. She was still chattering as they drove through the busy streets and finally on to the hotel.

The hotel foyer was all shiny glass and brass, polished wood and high ceilings. Jess looked down at her cheap jeans and felt slightly uncomfortable. As soon as she had the money from the will she vowed to splash out on some designer clothes. She watched as Giles walked up to reception and ordered afternoon tea to be brought up to the room – *awesome!*

They took the lift up to the first floor and walked the length of red carpet to their room. Once inside, Jess kicked off her shoes and sank her toes into the thick pile carpet, examined the opulence of the furnishings and the luxurious en suite. Giles, mildly amused, sat watching her on the large sofa under the window until a shadow fell across his face. He patted the seat beside him. 'Here. Come and sit down. I've got something to tell you.'

Her heart thumped against her ribs, her eyes wide. 'What? Don't say it's not true, that there is no will after all this.'

'No. There is a will, or rather a property trust. I've looked into it all.'

She sat down beside him and visibly relaxed. 'Phew! You gave me a fright there for a minute. What then? What've you found out?'

'It's quite a tangled web. Walter wanted to protect his assets; he didn't want his house and the grocery business falling into the wrong hands.'

'Why would they?'

'Well, Mary, his wife, was married before she met Walter and she already had a daughter from her previous marriage called Jean.'

'OK, so Jean wasn't his. And?'

'Let me finish! You're too impatient.'

Jess wanted to say, Huh, hark who's talking, but kept her lip buttoned.

'It seems that Jean and Mary were always at odds with Walter. When it came to his estate he wanted to protect it and leave it to his son, so he put his foot down.'

'Good for him. Sorry, go on.'

'He stated in the Property Protection Trust that the house and the money from his business empire were to go to his son, James. But as I think you know, he couldn't claim the estate until he was twenty-one but James died when he was nineteen. Walter had his wife certified insane and put into an asylum and he sold the house at Roundhay Park.'

'Blimey. But why would he sell his house?'

'I don't suppose we'll ever know but he was adamant that the proceeds went into the trust, claiming that his wife was of 'unsound mind' and could not be named as next of kin.'

'Gosh,' said Jess, 'things must've been bad.'

'Indeed, but it seems Jean contested the will after Walter's death.'

'That's Lydia's grandmother, right?'

'Correct.'

'What a shower!'

Giles looked off into the distance. 'Yes, it would appear that the women in that family have a lot to answer for.'

Jess was silent as she processed this information. Thank goodness Walter had his head screwed on otherwise she and Shelley would be none the wiser.

'There's something else.'

'OK, go on.' She felt a fresh wave of panic and stiffened.

'Your great-grandfather Walter...he committed suicide.'

Her first reaction was to brush it off. 'That's all right; it's not as if I knew him or anything.'

'No.'

But the more she thought about it the more she wanted to know. 'OK. You gonna tell me how?'

Giles took a deep breath. 'You really want to know?'

Jess nodded.

'He drowned himself in the lake in Leeds Park. He apparently left a note in his hat.'

Jess shivered. She was silent as she thought on this; she'd always had a fear of water. Swimming lessons at school were a no-no. She had always tried to get out of them saying she'd left her kit at home. 'Poor man. How did you find out?'

'His death certificate and the old newspaper obituaries.'

'Blimey, you have been busy.' Jess had a morbid curiosity to know more. 'Have you got the certificate? Can I see it?'

Giles went to his briefcase and searched through the documents he had acquired from the record office.

'I've always had a fear of water, funny, eh? I can't swim. I don't suppose I'll ever be able to go on your boat.'

Giles tried to lighten the mood. 'There is something called a life jacket.'

Jess smiled. 'Oh, yeah! Thanks for doing this for me. I always thought I came from such a poverty-stricken family, but now I know different.'

He handed her the document. She examined it slowly taking it all in and felt her blood run cold. 'Oh my God!'

'What is it?'

'That's my birthday! Walter committed suicide on the first of June.' She sat staring at the document. Her thoughts went back to a few sentences ago. 'You said he left a note. What did it say?'

'If I remember correctly, it went something like this: he couldn't live with himself after putting Mary away but he couldn't deal with any more of her evil accusations, ranting and raving about his escapades with other women, when all the time he'd been promoting and expanding his business to all hours. She was becoming violent, not only a danger to him but also to herself. He didn't know what else to do. There was no help in those days for people with mental illness other than an institution.

'It seems he'd built up his grocery empire from nothing; he was in the process of acquiring another store when their rows became even more bitter and frequent. These days she would be termed clinically depressed but Mary was committed to an asylum as insane. Walter wanted to make sure his son James inherited his estate, not Mary or Jean, so he put his estate into the property trust.'

'I never knew any of this. It's quite a story.'

'Yes. I wouldn't mind betting Lydia's inherited the insanity!'

Jess smiled – he'd actually made a joke!

Their traditional Yorkshire tea arrived on a trolley and the waitress wheeled it in front of the bay window. Giles gave her a tip and she left.

They both sat on the sofa in silent reflection while they enjoyed their tea consisting of tiny crustless sandwiches, scones, jam and cream and tiny iced fancies with a pot of Yorkshire tea.

Giles looked at Jess, 'I'll need to go over the documents with you and Shelley when she comes over. We'll need a witness, too.'

Jess dabbed her lips with a napkin and picked up her cup. 'Mandy'll do it. I'm picking Shelley up from Heathrow at three on Sunday afternoon.'

Giles nodded. 'There are a few things I thought we could do while we're here; we could explore Harrogate and maybe try and find Walter and Mary's house.'

'Yeah, Roundhay Park. Sounds good. I'd like to find Coverdale, too, if we've got time?'

'Ah, the painting.'

Jess nodded and looked at Giles. 'I think it's quite romantic about Walter's mother and the artist, Edward Clarke, don't you?'

'Her name was Emma.'

'Oh!' said Jess, 'like Emma Harte in *A Woman of Substance*!'

Giles looked blank.

'It's my favourite book.'

CHAPTER SEVENTEEN

On Thursday evening Eddie pulled up outside Jess's apartment and checked his appearance in the rear view mirror, ever hopeful that he could win her back. He'd made a special effort to remove the oily grime from his fingernails and put on his best jeans and tee shirt. He looked briefly at her car parked in the road and knocked on her door. No answer. He knocked again – maybe she was in the bathroom. Still no answer. He stood back from the door and scanned the upstairs windows for signs of life.

He heard someone shout, 'You're wasting your time, mate. There's no one in.'

Eddie turned to see a man leaning out of the downstairs window.

'You don't happen to know where she is?'

'No, mate. Sorry.'

Strange, but she couldn't have gone far. Her car was there. He decided to go round to Mandy's to see if she was there but he'd only been to Mandy's once and hoped he could remember the house.

He drove slowly down her road until he recognised the front garden that Mandy tended so well.

She was surprised to see Eddie standing on the doorstep.

'Hi. Is Jess there?'

'Oh, Eddie, she's gone up to Yorkshire for a few days.'

He frowned. 'Yorkshire? What for?'

This was tricky. Mandy didn't know if Jess had told him about the will. 'It was a spur-of-the-moment thing. She's gone to be with Giles.'

Eddie's face fell. 'Oh, right. Did she say when she'd be back?'

'I'm not sure. Look. Why don't you come in and I'll make you a cuppa.'

He looked at his watch. 'OK. Thanks.' He wiped his feet on the mat and followed Mandy through to the kitchen.

'Go and sit down, Eddie. I won't be a minute.'

He went through to the living room where Kirsty and Keira were playing on the floor with the kittens. He sat on the sofa and smiled at them; they smiled back shyly and giggled. He noticed the living room was cosily furnished, the sort of house he would have liked, but that was before…

Mandy came back with the tea and set it on the coffee table. 'Sugar?'

'No thanks. You've got a nice house, Mandy.'

'Thanks, we like it. We might put a conservatory on the back one day, when we've got the money.'

Eddie nodded and looked down at his mug of piping hot tea. 'Sort of place I had in mind for Jess and me.'

Mandy felt awkward. She would have to say something to Jess.

Buster and Sylvester started frantically chasing a ball of silver foil round the table legs with the twins trying to snatch it away from them.

'Oi, you two! Time you were getting ready for bed. You're getting too hyper.'

They chuckled and looked over at Eddie who forced a smile.

'I would've liked kids.'

'It's not too late. You're still young, Eddie.'

'Yeah, well...I need a partner first but it don't look like that's gonna happen.'

'You don't know that. There's plenty of girls out there but they ain't gonna come knocking on your door.'

Eddie sighed. 'It's Jess I want. I miss her.' He took a sip of tea. 'Is it serious with this Giles, then?'

'I can't really say, Eddie. Like I said, she's gone to meet him but I think it's more on business.'

His eyebrows shot up. 'Business?'

Mandy took a deep breath. 'I don't know if I should tell you. Hasn't Jess said anything?'

Eddie was on the edge of the sofa, his eyes wide. 'About what?'

'I think I ought to let her tell you... she's been looking into her family tree. It turns out her ancestors came from Yorkshire.'

'But I thought you said she went to be with this Giles?'

Mandy nodded.

Eddie looked blank. 'So?'

'He's helping her with the research. And it gave them an opportunity to escape the gossip.'

'Ah.' He waited for Mandy to give him more but she seemed reluctant to elaborate. 'What else?'

Mandy looked him in the eye, 'You'll have to ask her yourself.' She was sworn to secrecy about the will. She couldn't tell him.

'Why can't you tell me?'

'She told me not to tell anyone.'

'Not pregnant, is she?'

Mandy smiled and shook her head, 'No, nothing like that.'

Eddie blew out a sigh, 'Whereabouts in Yorkshire?'

'Leeds, I think, something to do with the Dales, too.'

'The Dales? I love it up there. I've always wanted to move to the country but whenever I've said this to Jess she never wants to leave London.' He finished his tea and put the mug back on the coffee table. 'So when's she coming home?'

'I told you, I don't know but I think they'll want to wait for all the publicity to die down.'

He stood up and looked down at his trainers. 'I see. Don't suppose there's much hope for me, then?'

Mandy shook her head and reached out to touch his arm, 'I'm sorry, Eddie.'

'Not as sorry as me.'

*

After a very lavish breakfast Giles escorted Jess to the centre of Harrogate. She was fascinated by the Victorian spa town with its high class shops and smart streets. She tried to imagine what it must have been like in Walter and Mary's day. Maybe there would have been little independent shops and emporiums like Walter's instead of the chains and big department stores, and probably horses and carts instead of cars. She imagined the ladies in their long skirts and big hats at the turn of the last century and wondered what Mary had looked like.

Giles took Jess to buy her some new clothes in one of the department stores. Jess knew what suited her but as Giles was paying she allowed herself the luxury of a personal shopper. The woman asked her size and what sort of things she was looking for and went to find suitable clothes. Jess was enjoying the whole experience and paraded up and down for Giles while he sat watching her on a sofa in the entrance to the dressing rooms. But he turned his nose up at the skimpy tight-fitting tops and shorts she chose and tried to persuade her to buy something tasteful. All the same, she was revelling in all this; she'd never had anyone spend copious amounts of money on her before, let alone someone like Giles.

After an hour Jess came out with more bags than she could carry so Giles asked for them to be delivered to the hotel. She couldn't stop smiling. Next, he suggested they have some lunch in *Auntie's* tea room. Jess suggested they find a pub but Giles said he didn't like town pubs. It became obvious to her that he was a stickler for staying in his comfort zone, so *Auntie's* it was.

They chose a table by the window overlooking the town. Jess noticed the tea room's Edwardian décor and the attention to detail: the wood panelling, vintage black and white photos of the town and local people on the walls, silver tea and coffee pots and doyleys on the elegant three-tier cake stands. Appetising home-made cakes stood under glass domes on the antique dresser. Each table was dressed with a white linen tablecloth and a cut-glass dish containing sugar cubes with delicate tongs in the silver lid. The waitress in black dress, white lacy cap and apron, came to take their order. It was like stepping back in time.

Their lunch consisted of dainty ham salad sandwiches with the crusts removed and a pot of Earl Grey, which Jess poured into mis-matched porcelain cups and saucers. A world away from the café Chris had taken her to!

'I'm looking forward to finding Walter's house,' said Jess, draining her cup.

Giles glanced at the school clock on the wall. 'Yes, if you've finished we'll make a move.'

'Just a minute,' said Jess, 'I want to have a look at the old photos.' She was hoping to get an idea of what Walter's shop had looked like. There was a picture of a grocer's shop in the high street with the shopkeeper dressed in a long white apron standing outside, his wares displayed in the window with the prices.

'Come on!' said Giles, 'it's getting late and the traffic will be building up.'

The city of Leeds was busy with multiple sets of traffic lights which Giles complained about. He turned on the sat-nav but he became more and more frustrated when it directed him down dead ends or down the wrong roads.

Jess couldn't believe how grumpy he was. 'Look, don't worry about it. I'll go another time.'

'No, we're here now. It should be in this area. Get the map out.'

Jess opened the glove box.

'No! Not in there! Behind your seat.'

'Gawd, you don't have to shout.' He was making her anxious and she wished he'd never suggested trying to find Roundhay Park. 'Stop the car.'

'What?'

'Stop the car. I think I saw a sign.'

Giles drew into the kerb a safe distance from the traffic lights and pulled the map towards him. 'Where the hell are we?'

She pointed to the place on the map. 'There.'

'But that's totally wrong.'

Jess blew out her cheeks. This was turning into a nightmare.

'Right, OK.' He gave the map back to her and shoved the S Class in 'drive'.

After another fifteen minutes in silence Jess was relieved when they eventually found Walter's address in Roundhay Park. While Giles parked the car in the tree-lined road Jess noticed all the houses were well cared for with large front gardens. Westwood was a detached red brick house surrounded by tall trees.

Jess got out of the car and stood at the wrought iron gate taking it all in. She tried to imagine what it would have been like to live there and once again was amazed at being descended from such a posh family. Beyond the gate set into an ornate brick wall, was a black and white chequered path leading to the porch with a pillar at each side. Two steps led to a large dark green front door furnished with an antique brass knocker and letter box. There were two big bay windows downstairs and two double sash windows upstairs. She wanted to knock and be shown around inside but Giles dissuaded her.

'I don't advise it. It could all look so different from what you imagine – some people modernise old houses, ripping out fireplaces and period features. You won't want to see that, will you? And another thing, we shouldn't intrude on these people. I already feel uncomfortable peering into their house.'

Ignoring his concerns, Jess was lost in her thoughts and wished she'd known Walter and Mary. She studied the house with its dark, foreboding exterior and wondered what events had taken place in there all those years ago. A cloud obscured the sun sending a shiver down her spine; she turned her back on the house and began to walk back to the car.

'Seen enough?' asked Giles, but she ignored him. He caught up with her. 'What's the matter?'

She already had her hand on the door handle. 'Nothing. Can we go now?'

'Of course, if that's what you want.'

On the way back to the hotel Jess sat in silence. She couldn't erase the unhappy-looking house from her mind. What had Walter and Mary really been like? There was no one alive who could tell her, apart from Lydia, and that was certainly a no-no. Jess tried to conjure up images of them; Walter in a three piece suit with a watch and chain in his waistcoat pocket and his wife, dressed in a long skirt, a high-neck blouse and hair piled up like Queen Mary. She imagined her stern expression when he was late home, demanding to know where he'd been. Maybe there was an element of truth in her suspicions? Jess would never know.

Back in the hotel room, Giles asked, 'Would you like to go out for something to eat tonight instead of eating in the hotel?'

Jess didn't answer. She felt strange after the odd experience of seeing Walter and Mary's house. She couldn't come to terms with the luxury they must have enjoyed up here in Leeds while her family had to watch every penny in London.

'Jessica?'

She had a lump in her throat. 'It's all so… unfair. They all had such cushy lives and we had to struggle to survive in that shitty council flat– we didn't know any of this existed,' she said, gesturing to the documents lying on the table.

He drew her to him and tilted her face up to his. 'You haven't answered my question. Do you want to eat out tonight?'

'Oh. No, sorry. I'm not in the mood. Can we eat here?'

He smiled at the difference between the two cousins. 'That's fine. I'm not in the mood either. I'll call room service later.'

Giles watched as she wandered over to the sofa and took out her new clothes and laid them on the sumptuous cream fabric. 'D'you wanna fashion show?'

'That would be nice,' he wriggled into a comfortable position on the bed and leaned back on one elbow, watching her.

Jess slipped off her jeans and started to unbutton her top, all the while conscious of his sultry gaze on her. 'What would you like to see?'

The sight of her undressing turned him on. 'Come here.'He pulled her onto the bed. She knelt over him with her blonde hair hanging down. He held a few strands to his lips before pushing her back on the bed. 'You can dress up for me later.'

The next morning at breakfast, they took their seats at one of the polished tables in the dining room and nodded 'good morning' to some of the other guests, just as they had the previous day. The waitress asked if they would like tea or coffee. Jess ordered coffee while Giles stuck to his usual tea. At the self-service buffet Jess felt like a child let loose in a sweet shop; she couldn't decide what to choose from all the fresh fruits, yoghurt, smoked salmon and croissants. She helped herself to some fruit compote and took it back to the table. The waitress came back with their coffee and tea and asked if they would like anything cooked. Giles declined but Jess plumped for a full English, toast and marmalade – she was going to make the most of everything that was on offer today. Giles settled for his usual muesli and a piece of fruit and shook his head at Jess. 'You'll never eat all that.'

'Just watch me – my stomach thinks me throat's cut.'

They had settled for a snack brought up to the room last night and she was now ravenous. While Jess began to tuck into the refreshing fruit, she noticed again the two tall, stone urns full of flowers placed in the centre of the room – the only time she'd seen anything like this had been in a garden but she really liked the idea of using them indoors. She also noticed the alcoves that lined the walls of the elegant dining room with a large watercolour of flowers in each. Beyond the open French doors was an outside seating area with wicker chairs and tables under a canopy of trees where she imagined enjoying a cappuccino in the dappled sunshine, if ever she got the chance. Giles was calling the shots on this trip but she was willing to go along with it, especially if it meant getting her hands on the will.

Giles was used to hotels of this calibre and didn't remark on any of the décor. As he ate his breakfast he told her they would drive out to the Dales directly. She had little idea how long the journey would be and hoped he wouldn't be in such a bad mood today.

Jess enjoyed being driven along the country roads in the purring S class, the sun bathing the countryside in golden light; such a pleasure after the dismal day in Leeds. She was surprised to find she enjoyed the open landscape of the Yorkshire dales with its little streams and miles and miles of dry stone walling. She'd never been anywhere like it before. Or had she? Yes, now she remembered! She had a vague recollection of going on a train journey with Nan and Dad one summer. It was a warm, sunny day. She and Shelley paddled in a little stream and they all sat on the grassy bank to eat their picnic that Nan had packed for them. Yes, it was slowly coming back to her now. Such a rare occasion but she remembered how happy she felt when the cool water flowed over her feet. Her dad had tried his hand with the fishing net and they all laughed when he only caught a few tadpoles. Yes. One of their happier times, how could she have forgotten that? She couldn't remember why they had taken this journey, or where it was; she had been very young and it was all very faint in her memory.

Giles suddenly parked the car. 'Let's have a walk. We'll be sitting a long time on the journey home and I need to stretch my legs.'

Jess said, 'Shouldn't that have been – *we* need to stretch *our* legs?'

He didn't answer but strode on ahead. She followed him along a grassy footpath, over stiles, through another field and through a kissing gate. It was certainly beautiful but Jess had never done so much walking and after a while her feet were complaining. 'Stop a minute. Me feet are killing me.'

'Well, you should've worn some sensible shoes not those silly things.'

She looked down at her pink party pumps now caked in mud and felt her anger rising. Eddie butted into her thoughts again – he would never have moaned at her, he would have laughed it off saying she was dressed up like a dog's dinner. What would he think if he saw her now? She remembered he had often talked of living in the country. She had always pooh-poohed the idea, but today, apart from her sore feet, she was enjoying the open fields, the fresh air and the birdsong.

They finally came across a bench and Jess sat down, peeled off her shoes and rubbed her aching feet. She would have given anything for a cup of tea but there was nothing for miles apart from two little cottages perched on the hillside amongst the trees.

Out of the blue, Giles said, 'So, Jessica, what are you going to do with your new-found wealth?'

She shrugged. 'Oh, I've got a few things lined up.'

'Yes but my advice would be to invest some of it.'

She wrinkled her nose. 'Spoken like a true lawyer.'

'No, think about it. Be guided by me; I've seen a lot of heartache where people have come into money and blown the lot and ended up with nothing again.'

'Yeah, right. I think I'd have a job to blow a million quid.'

'You may think so now, but believe me, I've seen it happen. A million isn't that much these days.'

'Not to you, maybe'.

'Look, all I'm saying is this, think about it.'

Boring old fart! Mandy was right. Doing all the things she'd always dreamed of was well within her grasp and no-one, not even Giles, was going to stop her. No, she wanted to enjoy her million when it finally landed in her lap. But after a while, her mind started to work on his advice. She could see the sense in it. What should she do? She didn't know anything about stocks and shares. She didn't want to put it away in some dusty old bank vault and hope it would earn interest. But she didn't want him always telling her what to do with *her* money either.

They started walking again and Jess was so deep in thought that she hadn't noticed the scene change before her. She stopped suddenly when she came upon the same view that Edward Clarke had captured on canvas. Coverdale, although the trees were different from the painting, looked even more beautiful in real life and Jess pictured Edward and Emma in the landscape. This was a totally different feeling to the one she'd had the day before. It was almost like coming home.

Giles noticed the change in her expression. 'Beautiful, isn't it?'

She nodded. 'I love it. I can picture Edward and Emma here all those years ago. Can we stay a bit longer? I dunno, it just feels right.'

'Of course. Stay as long as you want but remember I need to get back tonight.'

'I just want to get the feel of the place, sort of soak it up, you know?' She took some pictures on her phone, a 360 degree panorama of the woods with little clouds skittering across the bright blue sky. 'Would you like to live here?'

Giles shook his head. 'No. Too far from the sea.'

'Does it mean that much to you, then?'

'Oh, yes. It's everything to me. When I retire I'll be in Chichester permanently.'

Jess fell silent, she couldn't share his enthusiasm; she was becoming aware that they had two very different agendas. Wanting to relive that trip long ago she made her way to the stream, rolled up her skinny jeans and dipped her toes in the cool crystal clear water gurgling over the pebbles. The memory came flooding back and her heart sang. If only her Nan and her Dad were able to see her now.

CHAPTER EIGHTEEN

Jess finally got her wish and enjoyed sitting in the late afternoon sun on the terrace with a pot of tea. The fountain that trickled into the large clam-like dish in the centre of the patio had a soothing effect and she began to wish she could stay another night but they had to get back to London.

During the long journey the effects of the fresh air had Jess dozing in and out of sleep and dreaming about the next stage of her life. A plan was beginning to form in her mind. When she opened her eyes she noticed Giles complained bitterly about the other road-users overtaking him at more than seventy miles an hour.

She opened the glove box and searched for a CD but there weren't any so she turned on the radio.

'Turn that off! I can't concentrate,' said Giles.

Jess screwed up her face. She wished she'd brought her old MP3 player with her; she hadn't heard any music for days.

They had been on the road for over two hours and she was longing for a coffee and a wee.

Giles was locked in his own thoughts. He had felt out of control while he was away from the hub of his normality. He had an uneasy feeling, not knowing what was waiting for him at home. He hadn't had much contact with his father or Henry and he was hoping his divorce settlement had been taken care of and there wouldn't be any nasty shocks.

Jess shook him back to the present. 'Can we stop soon? I think I saw a sign for the services.'

'Whatever for? I hate those places.'

'Well, if you don't want a wet seat...'

He huffed, 'Oh, if you must.'

A big blue sign reared up in view. 'Here!' shouted Jess.

Giles reluctantly turned onto the slip road and into the services and found a parking space well away from all the other cars. 'Don't be long.'

After that remark Jess was going to take long as she wanted. Huh, who did he think he was? After making use of the ladies she sauntered over to the café for a cappuccino. She took her cardboard container full of steaming coffee to one of the tables. She sat blowing on it willing it to cool down.

A woman came and sat next to her. Jess wondered why when there were plenty of empty tables. The woman started talking but not actually to Jess.

'I've had to have me cat put down, at the vets. Not nice. Sad. I wonder what they do wiv 'em. Do they burn 'em?'

Jess noticed the woman had fake flowers in her hair scraped back in a pony tail. She wasn't young.

'Oh, dear,' said Jess, 'that is sad. What was wrong with him? Was he old?'

The woman looked at Jess as if she was an alien. 'Poor cat. I wonder what they do wiv 'em. Do they burn 'em?'

'I think they cremate them, yeah,' said Jess.

The woman started moving the salt and pepper around on the table and looking everywhere but at Jess.

Another woman came and sat down with a tray of drinks. 'Is she bothering you, dear?'

Jess shook her head. 'No, she's fine. So, she's had to have her cat put down, then?'

The woman nodded. 'But that was weeks ago. I'm sorry, dear, I'm her carer. She tends to pester people, especially when they're on their own.'

'Oh, it's not a problem. I expect she...'

'There you are! I've been looking everywhere. Come on,' said Giles, looking at his Rolex, 'you knew I wanted to get back,' and began to walk away.

Jess pulled a face at his back and the carer smiled knowingly. Jess snapped the lid on her coffee and took it with her. As they belted up Giles gave her a distasteful look and put the car in 'drive'. If it wasn't for the fact he was helping her with the will Jess wouldn't put up with this behaviour. She relaxed back in her seat and sipped her coffee, her mind on more exciting things.

*

It was very late when Giles opened the door to his apartment, Jess behind him. He put their bags down, turned slowly to Jess and whispered, 'I think 'you-know-who' is here.'

'Oh my God. You mean...?'

'Shhh!'

The wicked witch magically appeared in the hallway. 'Oh,' she said, looking from one to the other, 'I wondered when you were going to show up, you and the dozy blonde! You never cease to amaze me, Giles. How much do you know about her?'

Jess went to defend her character but Giles put his arm out to stop her. 'I know enough.'

Lydia spat venom. 'So, I was right! The little tart's got her feet well and truly under the table.'

'I want you to leave.'

Lydia threw her head back. 'Huh. This is my apartment now, you can't throw me out.'

'Yes I can. It's not yours yet and don't forget, I know the law.'

'You! You and your scheming father have done me out of thousands. He's been a very busy boy this week.'

'It's your own fault.'

Jess couldn't stand by and watch this happen. 'Just a minute, don't talk as if I'm not here. I'm not a dozy blonde or a tart, for your information. You've probably got more money than I'll ever see but at least I've got manners!'

Lydia's jaw dropped at Jess's outburst. She stared at her like a crazy woman. 'Oh, the tart has a voice.'

'Listen, I may have come from a poor family but they were richer in warmth and kindness than yours will ever be!'

'You know nothing about my family.'

'Ha, that's what you think.'

Giles intervened; he didn't want Lydia finding out about Jessica's connections and he was also frightened this could turn into a cat-fight. 'Don't upset yourself, Jessica. She's not worth it.'

'Oh, I suppose it's luurve is it? Well my dear, you're welcome to him.' She turned to Giles, 'And you haven't heard the last of this.' She left the apartment banging the door behind her. For a brief moment, Giles was reminded of Jessica doing the same thing not so long ago.

'Now you can see what I'm up against,' said Giles.

'Blimey. I'd forgotten how bad she was.'

'I just want that bitch out of my life. Forever.'

He strode to his study and started going through the papers on his desk. Jess stood in the doorway watching him. 'What do you think she was doing here?'

Without looking up at her, Giles said, 'Probably looking for some more ammunition to use on me; all the drawers are open.'

'How come? Don't you keep them locked?'

'Yes, but she's got her own set of keys. She wouldn't have found any important documents here anyway, Jacob will have seen to that before he left. They'll all be in the office safe.'

'Didn't you realise she'd go through all this stuff?'

He was irritated at Jessica's accusation but reproached himself for the oversight. 'I know. I should have had the locks changed. I meant to do it ages ago.'

Jess felt quite smug and in control. 'Anyway, leave that. I'll get us something to eat, I'm starving.'

He turned and gave her the first smile of the day. 'That would be nice. I can't believe you've come from the same stable as that bitch.'

*

After breakfast the following morning, Giles offered to take Jess to the airport but she refused – she wanted to do this her way. It was going to be wonderful seeing Shelley again after twelve years and she wanted her sister all to herself. Jess had never been to Heathrow before but she'd Googled it and it seemed pretty straightforward. She recited it in her head. Terminal five, park in the multi-story and go to the arrivals lounge, watch the screens for information.

'I'll drive you home when you're ready,' said Giles.

'Thanks. It's been so long since I've seen her I've forgotten what she looks like. Maybe I ought to carry a sign saying 'Jess' in big letters!'

'You'll be fine.'

They arrived outside Jess's apartment late morning. She asked him in but he declined. 'I'll leave you to it. I'd hate you to be late picking her up,' he said, knowing how easy it was for her to become distracted. Then, as an afterthought, 'Don't forget – tell Shelley and Mandy to be at my office 9 o'clock sharp on Tuesday morning.'

Jess shot upstairs and dumped her holdall in the bedroom. Something told her to check her emails. Oh My God! Shelley had left a series of messages over the last few days. She checked her phone and listened to the last message on there. 'God, where are you, Jess? I've been phoning all week. My flight time's been changed again; rocking up now at 13.30 on Sunday. Let me know if you can't get there – I'll get a taxi.'

Jess grabbed her car keys, jumped in her car and drove straight to Heathrow. She managed to find the multi-storey, remembered to make a note of the level she was on and hurriedly followed the signs to the arrivals lounge. She glanced at her watch; a quarter past one, just time to grab a coffee. She queued impatiently hoping she had time to drink it. She sat down and glanced up at the screen and followed the long list of flights. One stood out from all the others:

'Flight VA525 from Sydney – LANDED'

She took her coffee and headed towards the barrier. What she saw reminded her of the opening scene from 'Love Actually': People filtering through with trolleys full of luggage, tears of joy as they hugged their partners, friends and relations.

But no Shelley.

Suddenly, Jess spotted a tanned outdoorsy-looking woman on her own dressed in khaki shorts, tee shirt and sandals, her sun-streaked hair in a pony tail, pushing a trolley piled up with cases.

'Shelley?'

The woman scanned the queue for the source of the voice. Her face lit up, 'Jess! Geez, I thought I was on my own there for a minute.'

Jess put down her coffee, ran to Shelley and hugged her. She stood back. 'Wow! Let me look at you!'

They were both giggling and hugging each other, tears on both their faces.

'It's so good to see you, you're looking great.'

'So are you.'

'Blimey Shel, I've been away for a few days and only got your message this morning.'

'Cripes! You were cutting it fine, where've you been?'

'Yorkshire. Come on, I'll tell you on the way. Oh, hang on – you OK? Need the loo or a coffee?'

'Nah, I'm fine, just bushed.'

In the car, Jess put on her CD of Duran Duran and Shelley looked sideways at her, 'God! You don't still listen to that stuff?'

Jess grinned. 'I just thought it'd bring back a few memories. You used to drive poor Nan and Dad ballistic, what with that and Madonna.'

'Yeah, I did, didn't I?'

'Giles hates it.'

'Ah well, can't please everyone.'

They sat in silent reflection as Jess drove out of the airport. Where had those years gone? It seemed like yesterday.

When they were on the open road she filled Shelley in on the events leading up to today.

Shelley said, 'So, when am I gonna meet this Giles guy?'

'Tuesday, at the document signing.'

They grinned at each other; Shelley punched the air. 'Yesss! Can't wait!'

'Me neither.'

'There's such a lot I wanna do while I'm here, Jess. I've made a list.'

'Wicked!'

Shelley slumped in the passenger seat, her head lolled forward and her eyes closed. Jess was once again lost in thought until they arrived outside her apartment. She helped Shelley with her luggage and locked the car.

'I like your fun pink car, Jess.'

'Thanks. Got it insured with *Sheila's Wheels*, too.'

'Good girl!'

They struggled upstairs with the cases, dumped them on the living room floor and Jess headed straight for the kettle. 'Cuppa?'

'Oh, mate! Lifesaver. Got any Earl Grey?'

'Not sure.' She rummaged in her cupboard. 'No, sorry. I'll pop round the shop if you like?'

'Nah, leave it for now. I'll make do with water.' Shelley sank heavily on the sofa. 'God I'm bushed. Twenty-four hours on that bloody plane...' She looked around at Jess's living room. 'Nice little place you got here. Similar to mine in Oz. Don't suppose I could have a shower?'

'Course. Help yourself. What's mine is yours.'

While Shelley was in the shower, Jess rang Mandy who told her the bed had been made up for a week and the room was all ready. She could hardly hear herself think with the twins jumping up and down and shouting in the background, so excited were they at the thought of having another 'auntie' to stay. But Mandy was still not happy with the way Jess had treated Eddie. She couldn't let it go.

'He came round to check your tyres on Thursday evening – did you forget?'

'Oh my God! What did he say?'

'He was more upset than anything. He really loves you, Jess.'

Jess sighed.

'I think you owe him. You're supposed to be friends, aren't you?'

'Yeah, you're right. I'll phone him.'

Mandy was pleased. 'Yeah, you should. Anyway, how's Shelley?'

'Fine, she's in the shower. Listen, I've got no food in Mandy. I feel awful, it's not like me. It was such a rush, coming back from Greenwich and then straight to Heathrow. What am I gonna do?'

'Don't even think about it; I'll rustle something up. See you both later.'

At Mandy's, Jess and Shelley were treated like movie stars. It seemed Mandy had pulled a lavish feast out of thin air. She produced a chicken salad and a bottle of wine, which Shelley was devouring at a rate of knots in between telling them all about Australia and showing them photos. They were all caught up in the infectious excitement and anticipating the signing of the documents on Tuesday until Mandy asked the twins to go and help her in the kitchen. There was a lot of excited chatter and laughter with Mandy trying to keep them quiet. It was obvious they would be treated to a surprise and very soon all three of them emerged carrying a birthday cake in the shape of a pink handbag with lighted candles and mini sparklers stuck in it. They placed it carefully on the table.

Mandy was all smiles. 'Happy birthday!'

'Make a wish, Auntie Jess!' said Keira

'Yes, go on!' shouted Kirsty.

'OK, but it's not my birthday till Tuesday.'

'Wait a minute; you haven't got thirty candles on that cake.' said Shelley.

The twins looked at each other, 'We couldn't fit them all on.'

Shelley winked. 'Only joking.'

'What you going to wish for, Auntie Jess?' asked Kirsty.

Mandy jumped in, 'You mustn't ask that. It's bad luck.'

This time last year Jess would have known exactly what to wish for but her life had taken on such a tremendous transformation these past few weeks she hardly knew herself. She had a picture in her mind's eye but she wasn't going to tell anyone, not even Mandy. Not yet. She blew out the candles and wished.

CHAPTER NINETEEN

Holding hands, Jess and Shelley smiled at each other and ran through department store's main entrance into the lobby. The last time they set foot in the store they had been children, chased away by a store detective telling them never to return.

They looked around. It was all still as they remembered – the marble floor, the big chandeliers, the skylight...

'Well, Jess. How's it feel?'

'Awesome! I never dreamed I'd be setting foot in here again, let alone going for afternoon tea...'

'...or in my case, breakfast. Crikey, I'd forgotten all about jet-lag. Sorry I didn't surface this morning.'

'No problem.'

They took the escalator up to the tea room on the third floor and chose a table. As she sat down, Jess was surprised to find the furniture and décor weren't quite what she expected. She thought it looked a bit shabby. While they waited to be served, she told Shelley that Giles had been on the phone earlier and was disappointed that she wasn't going to be spending the evening with him.

'Oh, mate, that's why I'm still single; I can't be doing with all that nonsense. I like my freedom too much.'

'Haven't you ever wanted to settle down, Shel?'

'Yeah, I've tried it a couple of times but never again; I'd rather eat dog poo and set myself on fire!'

Jess collapsed in peels of laughter. 'Oh, Shel. It's so good to be with you again.'

'Don't want no ankle-biters, neither.'

'What?'

'Kids.'

Jess nodded. 'Oh.'

'Well, Jess, you have to weigh it up, but in the end it always comes down to the same thing. You know me; I hate restriction.'

Jess knew only too well. 'Yeah, I can remember Dad always telling you off for being late home.'

'Yeah, and Nan always wanting me to help in the kitchen, but I'd bunk off!'

'Good times.' Jess was thoughtful. She lowered her voice to a whisper. 'I just think it's amazing that we've come into all this money. What you gonna do with yours?'

'God! I don't even have to think about that. Go round the world, of course.'

'Oh, right.' Jess was a little hurt at the tactless way in which Shelley had come out with it. Didn't she want to spend some time with her sister?

'What about you, Jess? Got any plans?'

'I'm working on it. Giles said I should invest some of it; maybe some sort of business.'

'Weren't you with someone called Eddie? What happened to him?'

Jess looked down at her lap. 'It sort of fizzled out.'

Shelley raised one eyebrow as if she wanted an explanation.

'Look. I didn't want the same sort of life we had as kids, OK? I hated that Nan and Dad never knew where the next penny was coming from. Eddie...well.'

Shelley nodded. 'But you still like London?'

'Yeah, Eddie kept talking about getting out of London. I didn't want that; I didn't think that was the answer.'

'Well, from what I've seen of it he's got the right idea.'

'You've changed your tune.'

Shelley smiled. 'One thing Australia's taught me is that you have to move on, Jess. Grab life with both hands. You're a long time dead.'

A grey-haired waitress came to take their order. She looked them up and down. 'I'm afraid you can't sit here; this table is reserved for one of our regular customers.'

Jess and Shelley looked at each other. This wasn't on. After all these years, nothing had changed.

'Look, our money's as good as the next person's,' said Shelley.

'I'm sure it is, madam, but I've got strict instructions to reserve this table for Mrs Morgan.'

Jess turned white. *Morgan? Oh my God.*

Shelley was alarmed. 'What is it, Jess?'

The waitress looked around for the management to relieve her of this difficult situation. She hoped these two women weren't going to cause trouble.

'I'll tell you outside. Come on, Shel, I'm not staying here.'

Shelley followed Jess leaving the grey-haired waitress looking aghast.

Jess hurried to the escalator and glanced behind her. 'I don't know if it's Mrs Morgan junior or senior, but I'm not hanging around to find out!'

Shelley was trying to keep up. 'What the hell are you talking about?'

Jess stopped dead and faced Shelley. 'Oh my God. Look. I think it's either Giles's wife or his mother; if it's Cruella I don't want to be anywhere near her, especially after Saturday night.'

'That bad, eh?'

'Worse, and to top it all off, she's our cousin!'

'Geez! You're right. I'd forgotten about that.'

They walked out of the store and realised that it didn't really measure up to their expectations, anyway.

'Where to now?' asked Jess.

'Harvey Nix?'

'Yeah, come on.'

In Harvey Nichols, Jess couldn't stop smiling over the celebration tea. There were smoked salmon and crab finger sandwiches, fruity scones with clotted cream and salted caramel sauce, and a selection of little cakes and a bottle of champagne.

'Good tucker,' said Shelley, sliding another finger sandwich into her mouth and licking her fingers. 'Don't know if I can do it justice, though.'

'Don't worry, I'll ask for a doggie bag.'

'You can't do that!'

'Yeah? Watch me.' She called the waiter over. 'This is delicious.'

The waiter smiled. 'Thank you, madam. We endeavour to please.'

'Yeah, it's just we don't think we'll be able to eat it all. Can we take the cakes home?'

'Of course, I'll see to it straight away.' He took the three-tier cake stand away and was back in a flash with a presentation box tied up with a pink ribbon. 'There we are, madam. No extra charge.'

'I should think not!' said Shelley.

They drank the last of the champagne and chuckled at the bubbles tickling their noses. Jess was revelling in the luxury of the whole experience but Shelley was less than impressed. She found London tired and dirty and kept comparing it with Sydney. 'You got a passport, Jess? I'd love to show you Sydney. Who knows? You might love it as much as I do and end up staying. We could buy a house together; it's a totally different life.'

'Hang on – I thought you were going round the world?'

'Oh, yeah, I forgot!'

'Don't forget to get up in the morning. If you're not up by seven-thirty, I'll come round and drag you out of bed.'

'Yeah, no worries there. I won't forget that.'

Back at Mandy's they gave the box of cakes to the twins to share. Their eyes popped out when they opened the box. 'Ooh, thank you,' they said in unison.

'Yeah, thanks. That was a lovely gesture,' said Mandy.

Trevor came to see what they'd been given. 'Oh, man. Save some for me!'

'You can have them tomorrow, after tea,' Mandy told the twins, 'you've just cleaned your teeth.'

They took the box and set it in pride of place on the sideboard and put their hands behind their backs. They looked at Jess and Shelley with cheeky smiles and Jess felt her heart would burst with love.

*

Jess had just come back from leaving Shelley at Mandy's when she heard a knock at the door. She ran down the stairs and was surprised to see Eddie standing there. 'Oh, hi Eddie,' she felt ashamed after what Mandy had told her. She still hadn't phoned him. 'Come in.'

Eddie looked as awkward as she felt as he followed her upstairs. 'I had to see you, Jess. I hope you don't mind.'

'I'm sorry I wasn't here on Thursday. I was in Yorkshire.'

'Yeah, I know. Mandy said.'

She led him into the open plan living room. 'Have a seat, Eddie. Do you wanna drink?'

'Er, OK. Thanks.'

'Tea?'

'Yeah, fine.' He sat on the edge of the sofa looking down at his feet, hands resting on his knees.

Jess shouted from the kitchenette, 'So, what did Mandy tell you?'

'Oh, just that you were escaping the gossip and doing some family history or something. Look, what's this all about?'

Jess wasn't sure how much to tell him. She came back with his cup of tea and put it on the coffee table.

'I'm worried about you, Jess. What's going on?'

'There's nothing to worry about. I'm fine.'

'What's all this?' he said, looking at the cup and saucer. 'Bit posh innit?''

Jess smiled. 'Not really. I like using a cup and saucer.'

Eddie raised his eyebrows. 'What's happening to you Jess? I don't know you anymore.'

It was no good. She had to tell him. 'I've got something to tell you.'

'Huh, oh yeah? I s'pose you're getting married to this Giles character?'

Jess wanted to laugh. She shook her head. 'No, it's something much better than that,' she could hardly contain herself.

'What, then?'

She bounced on the sofa beside him with a broad, wide-eyed grin. 'I've come into money, Eddie!'

He sat gaping at her, stunned. 'You're joking, right?'

Jess shook her head. 'Nope, it's true. It's a long story but Shelley wrote to me a couple of weeks ago. She's over from Australia.'

'Bloody hell!' Eddie took a gulp of his tea and nearly choked. When he'd recovered he asked, 'So what you gonna do?'

'Not sure yet. I'm working on it. I haven't got the money yet; there's been a lot to sort out.'

'Christ. How much?'

Jess couldn't stop smiling, 'Over a million.'

'What, between you?'

'No, each.'

'Bloody hell, Jess,' Eddie's brain was swimming. 'So, where's your sister now?'

'At Mandy's; she's putting her up. We've got to go to Giles's office tomorrow and sign the documents – all of us, Mandy's witness.'

So this is what Mandy couldn't tell him. He put the cup and saucer on the coffee table and turned to Jess. 'I'm really pleased for you, love. It's what you've always wanted.' He picked up her hand and kissed it, gave it a squeeze. There was a weak smile playing around his mouth. 'And you don't need no geezer with money.'

Jess beamed. 'I know.'

Eddie glowed as it all started to sink in. He was still in with a chance. 'This calls for a celebration!' he said, looking at his watch. 'Tell you what... I'll take you out tomorrow night, all right?' Then a cloud passed over his face, 'Unless you're going out with bloody Giles?'

She decided to keep him guessing. 'Nothing planned at the moment.'

'What? You mean he's not taking you out to celebrate? What kind of bloke is he?'

'A rich one.'

'But you haven't told me much about him. How does he fit into all this?'

'He's done some of the research into the will, that's all. It's a bit complicated. Briefly, after Shelley and I looked into our family history, we found out we're related to his estranged wife.'

'No! How come?'

'It's a long story.'

'So? I'm not going anywhere.'

Jess told Eddie the whole story and two cups of tea later he was looking more relieved. 'So, what did you think to the Dales?'

'Oh, I love it, Eddie. Can't wait to go back. It felt so right, you know?'

'Really?'

'Yeah, it felt like ...like home.'

Eddie let this last remark sink in then asked, 'So, do you think you'll end up living there, then?'

She nodded. 'I hope so. I think Shelley's right – you have to move on; grab life with both hands.'

'And erm...what about Giles?'

Jess took a while to answer; that was the leading question. She couldn't picture life with him, his moods and his controlling ways. She couldn't see Giles falling in with what she wanted to do either. The trip to Yorkshire had truly opened her eyes. But she didn't want to sound too eager where Eddie was concerned.

'I don't know, Eddie. It's all a bit soon to think about that.'

Eddie was dying to ask if he was in with a chance but Jess cut him short.

She stood up, 'God, is that the time? I've got stuff to sort out and it's a busy day tomorrow.'

He walked to the door, turned and kissed her, taking her by surprise. It was the kind of kiss that stirred in her a long-forgotten deep emotion. She had never felt like this with Giles. Mandy's words came back to her. *He really loves you, Jess.*

'I'll see you tomorrow night, don't forget,' then he added, 'by the way, your hair looks good.'

Eddie left with a spring in his step. All was not lost; he started to make some plans of his own. And as for that bloke Giles... he sounded a bit of a tosser by all accounts – bloody sailing? Didn't he realise what he had in Jess? Anyway, his loss. Eddie couldn't believe it could all work out for him; it just needed a bit of tact and diplomacy. There was no point in coming on strong; that, he knew, would never work with Jess. He had to take a few steps back and let her come to the same conclusion that he had, a long time ago.

*

On Tuesday morning Lydia arrived at Morgan Bishop and barged straight past The Mouse who told her Giles was in a meeting, and burst into his office crashing the door to one side.

'Thanks to you, my business has gone bust!' she blurted out. 'You and your father have had a hand in this, I know it.'

A blanket of silence fell on the room. Giles and his father glared at her. Jess, Shelley and Mandy sat open-mouthed at the scene unfolding before them.

Lydia glanced at the papers spread out in front of Giles and Jacob and turned to see the three women sitting at the table. 'Oh. And what have we here? A regular little coffee morning. Very cosy.'

'Lydia, please,' said Jacob, 'this is a private matter.'

'I bet it is!' Her dark eyes flashed at Jess. 'And what's *she* doing here?'

'It's none of your business,' said Giles, 'now, please leave or I'll have you forcibly removed.'

'She's getting the money I'm entitled to, is that it?'

'Of course not, I told you, this has nothing to do with you.'

'You can't fool me, I know her type. What's the matter with you Giles? Can't you see what she's doing?'

Shelley couldn't sit back and say nothing. 'If you must know, we've been researching our family history and found out that we've inherited a legacy.'

'Huh! A likely story.'

'It's true,' said Giles, 'I've looked into it myself.'

'You? You couldn't look into a mirror!'

Shelley was astounded and said to Jess, loudly, 'I can't believe she's related to us. We were brought up with manners!'

Lydia looked like someone had smacked her in the face with a wet fish. 'Related? Don't be ridiculous, how could you ever be related to me?'

Jess joined in. 'I'd rather you weren't, but unfortunately, we share the same great-great-grandfather.'

'All right, what was his name?'

'Walter Nelson, he lived in Leeds and owned a chain of grocers' stores before the war. We're cousins.'

'I don't believe you, there must be some mistake.'

'No, Lydia,' said Jacob, calmly. 'There's no mistake.'

A cunning grin settled on her face, her nose in the air. 'Well, in that case I must be entitled to part of the will.'

'Sorry, it doesn't work like that. It comes down through the male line,' said Giles.

'This is all a conspiracy to ruin me!' she started towards the door. 'You'll be hearing from my solicitor.'

'There's nothing you can do. It's all completely legal and water tight,' said Jacob.

Jess was relieved. *Thank God.*

'We'll see about that,' spat Lydia, and stormed out of the room.

All three women looked at each other and heaved a sigh of relief.

Giles was thankful his soon-to-be-ex had gone and that he and Jacob had worked as a team. 'Now, where were we?'

Jacob smiled and said, 'Yes, if you can all sign on the dotted line….'

The business completed, Jess and Shelley gave each other a high five. 'Yesss!' hissed Jess.

'I'm so pleased for you both,' said Mandy, 'and I hope that's the last you see of *her.*'

'My sentiments exactly!' said Giles. 'Now, if you're ready? I'm taking all three of you out to lunch.' Giles spoke into the intercom, 'Gloria, have Benson bring the Mercedes round to the front, would you?'

Jess glowed with pride, Mandy was happy for her and Shelley was lapping it up.

All three sat in the back of the S Class with beaming smiles, relieved they had dressed up for the occasion – Giles hadn't told them they would be dining at a posh restaurant – and Jess joked that the royal family had nothing on them. Giles sat in the front seat and Benson drove the car smoothly through the traffic towards the Strand.

Giles turned to them. 'I'm sure you'll love the place I'm taking you to. It holds very special memories for me; my parents used to take me there as a child.'

All three women grinned and clutched hands.

They arrived outside Thompson's, a well established restaurant with a history going back 150 years. Benson dropped them off and drove away.

Giles escorted them through to the lobby and a waiter appeared from nowhere. Giles slipped a roll of notes into his top pocket, 'My usual table please, Max.'

'Certainly, Mr Morgan.' He scanned the seating area and said, 'If you would care to relax in the bar, sir? I'll be a few moments,' and hurried away. There were some diners at the table Giles had requested and Max quickly moved them to another one.

Shelley whispered to Jess, 'Crikey. Did you see that? It's like James Bond.'

When they were seated at their table, Giles asked Max for the wine list and ordered a bottle of their finest Pinot Grigio.

Mandy noticed the price tag of the Chateauneuf du Pape and nudged Jess in the ribs; the cost would have fed her family for a week. Trevor would never believe her.

Max came back with the wine, showed the bottle to Giles who nodded confirmation. Max ceremoniously opened the bottle and poured a little into a glass for Giles to taste. He picked it up, took in the bouquet, swirled it around and took a sip. All three women sat transfixed and tried to keep a straight face. Giles nodded to Max who then poured four glasses with a flourish.

Giles took the initiative, 'Happy birthday, Jessica.'

They all chinked glasses. 'Yeah, happy birthday!' they all chimed.

Jess observed the wood panelling, crisp white tablecloths and chandeliers. Thompson's was known for the best roast beef and lamb in the country, carved at guests' tables from antique silver domed trolleys. To think that when Jess and Shelley were children, eating their minced beef in gravy, Giles had been enjoying this rich fare. He proudly went on to tell them about the famous people in history who had dined there including Vincent van Gogh, Charles Dickens, Benjamin Disraeli and William Gladstone.

A pianist started to play and Mandy was just about to say 'old fart's music' but bit her tongue when she saw the shiny grand piano. She was slowly beginning to realise what Jess had been experiencing and what it had meant to her.

Shelley was silently taking it all in; she'd never been anywhere like this. A stroke of luck finding this Giles fella; from the look of things, he was a handy bloke to have around.

They all sat perusing their menus while Giles explained that the restaurant was known for its roast beef hung for twenty eight days.

'Sounds good to me,' said Shelley.

'Yes please,' said Mandy, 'It's like Sunday roast, only better.'

Giles looked at Jess. 'How about you, Jessica? I know lamb is your favourite.'

'You remembered. Mm, I love lamb, but if Thompson's is known for its beef…'

Giles called Max over and ordered four plates of roast beef. He established how they would like it cooked and went directly to the kitchen.

Giles observed all three women; they couldn't have been more different from each other. Jessica, with her model-girl looks and sense of fun, her sister, the natural outdoor-bred Aussie, and Mandy, the mother hen who always had Jessica's best interests at heart. He couldn't have envisaged doing this six weeks ago. But he was aware of a slight reticence and thought he ought to start the conversation. He asked Shelley how she liked being back in England.

'It's great. Jet-lag's a bugger though, especially with a couple of glasses of wine on top, and I can't get used to the water going down the plughole the wrong way.'

They all found this amusing.

'That's something you don't think about, isn't it?' said Giles.

'Yeah, the sun comes up on the opposite side, too.'

'Really.' Not being good with small talk, Giles was searching for something else to say and could only think to ask Shelley what line of work she was in.

'Oh, I'm a tour guide for Sydney tourism. It's great; so many good things about Australia but probably the best is the amazing beaches and if you're into water sports, that's the place to be.'

Giles's face lit up. 'What about sailing?'

'Oh, mate, now you're talkin'!' She took a sip of wine and continued. 'Yeah, most weekends I can crew on a boat for someone, if I want. Racing's fantastic; a real big yachting fraternity, down under.'

'Sounds wonderful. Jessica never told me you were into sailing.'

'Probably forgot to tell her, there's been so much happening.'

Jess joined in. 'Giles has got a yacht at the Solent, haven't you?'

His eyes never left Shelley. 'That's right, a Moody 31. She's moored in Chichester harbour. Got a boathouse there, too.'

'Fantastic. They're a lovely boat. A mate of mine's got one; he calls her Rosie.' Shelley was really getting into her stride now. 'Do you get down there much?'

'Not as often as I'd like.' Giles started to tell Shelley all about Sea Witch, the boathouse, the Chichester area and his yacht club on the Thames and made it sound very attractive. But Jess, of course, had heard it all before and was beginning to find the whole thing a bit tedious.

Their roast beef arrived on an antique silver domed trolley and the chef endeavoured to carve the meat in front of them; the training for this, Giles told them, takes weeks to perfect. Jess was totally fascinated. Her thirtieth birthday was turning out to be one she would never forget.

Someone's mobile was ringing; they all looked at each other then Jess realised it was hers. 'Oh my God, it's Chris! I was supposed to phone him.' She excused herself and went to answer the call in the lobby.

Chris wanted to know how she had been getting on and when she would be able to return to work. 'All three shops are really busy, Jess; it must be all the publicity. I would really like you to come back as soon as possible. I've had customers asking for you by name.'

She felt flattered but she couldn't tell him about the will over the phone. 'OK. Tomorrow soon enough?'

'Tomorrow would be excellent. See you at nine.'

When Jess returned to the table, Giles, Shelley and Mandy were halfway through their meal. Giles and Shelley were engrossed in conversation together and Mandy was relieved to see Jess; she gave her a look that spoke volumes. 'So, what did Chris want?'

Helping herself to some vegetables, Jess proceeded to eat her meal. 'Oh, he wants me back at work tomorrow; they're really busy. I told him I'd be there. Well, what could I say? I couldn't tell him about the will, not on the phone.'

Mandy, with a mouthful of roast beef, answered with a shrug of her shoulders.

Their meal was delicious. They all enjoyed the ceremony of it and Giles couldn't remember a time when he had enjoyed himself so much. He was totally caught up in the convivial atmosphere and Shelley was so knowledgeable about everything to do with sailing, he'd never met a woman like her. Caught up in the excitement, he suddenly put his knife and fork down, took a sip of wine and said, 'I've just had an excellent idea. Why don't all three of you join me at the boathouse tomorrow? There's plenty of room and I know Jessica's been dying to see it, haven't you?'

Jess was speechless. She smiled and nodded then looked at Mandy who said, 'I'd love to, but I'm sorry, I've got family commitments. Maybe another time?'

Giles nodded, 'Of course,' then he turned his gaze back to Jess and waited for her answer.

Jess tried to make her reason sound valid. 'Sorry I can't either, Chris is expecting me back at work tomorrow. People have been asking for me by name, the office is really busy at the moment and I don't want to let him down.'

But she was knocked sideways when Giles chinked glasses with Shelley and said, 'Well, Shelley, looks like it's just you and me.'

'Sounds great!' said Shelley but winced when it dawned on her what she had agreed to. 'Sorry, Jess. Don't mind, do you? Maybe you can join us later, at the weekend?'

Mandy gave Jess one of her aren't-you-going-to-do-something looks. This couldn't be happening, surely?

'Yeah, sure,' said Jess, her appetite rapidly waning. She pushed the last of her roast beef to one side with her knife.

Mandy felt uncomfortable about all this. She looked at her watch and said, 'Actually I've got to get back to pick the twins up from school.'

Giles rang for Benson to take Mandy home and continued talking animatedly to Shelley.

Benson appeared at the door. Mandy got up to leave and gave Shelley and Giles a sharp look. She whispered to Jess, 'I'll catch you later.'

Jess nodded and forced a smile. The occasion had fallen a bit flat.

Giles was oblivious to the fact that he'd upset Jess. He continued talking to Shelley about Cowes week at the beginning of August and some foreign place Jess had never heard of and she started drifting off into her own world. A vision of Eddie swam before her eyes; she replayed how she felt when he'd kissed her last night, making her glow and her heart swell. She looked at Giles with his expensive clothes and remembered his moods and how awkward he had made her feel in the Dales. Her mind was going into overdrive.

Shelley was throwing her head back and laughing. Giles was in his element; he'd never met a woman like Shelley. He was now telling her about Europe's biggest yachting festival at La Rochelle. The two of them were bubbling over with excitement.

Giles suddenly turned to Jess. 'So, what do you think, Jessica?'

Jess snapped back to the present. 'Sorry, what?'

Giles was wondering if Jessica was the woman for him, after all. He observed Shelley; her natural, earthy looks and easy-going nature; *she* wouldn't complain about her aching feet. And Jessica like a supermodel straight out of a fashion magazine. The two sisters were poles apart. 'I was just saying to Shelley, all three of us could go to La Rochelle next year.'

'What for?'

'Weren't you listening?'

'No, sorry. Zoned out.'

'There's a huge boating festival in France... I thought we could all go?'

'Yeah, OK, sounds cool.'

Giles started on about it again but it wasn't holding Jess's attention. She was too busy working out a plan for her investment.

ONE YEAR LATER

Jess's heart swelled with pride. Bright sunlight shone through the Georgian windows and highlighted the antique brass bedstead and white Egyptian cotton bed linen. White walls reflected the light and two large Indian rugs graced the wooden floor.

Mandy, Trevor and the twins were coming to stay for Jess's birthday and she could hardly contain her excitement. The thought of Kirsty and Keira running upstairs giggling, bouncing on the beds, spurred her on to apply the finishing touches that made the rooms extra special. She was also anticipating the look on Mandy's face when she saw the extent of her creative skills. Jess made sure everything was just right, checked the other bedrooms and bathrooms looked equally amazing and finally went downstairs.

Bracken Farmhouse was her venture that she had been working towards, throwing all her time, expertise and energy into it. The day after the lunch at Thompsons, Jess couldn't wait to tell Chris about her good fortune. He sent her home at once and said although he would miss her sunny disposition, he was over the moon for her and said it couldn't happen to a nicer person.

'Well, if you need any help finding a suitable property…or a surveyor…'

'Thanks, Chris.'

'Don't mention it. Let me know how you get on. You have my very best wishes.'

'If you're ever in the Dales you must drop in, once I get myself sorted of course.'

'My dear girl, try keeping me away!'

When she arrived home that morning, Shelley had already left for the Solent but Jess decided her time was better spent making plans rather than joining her sister and Giles.

She immediately booked a B&B in the Dales with a view to spending some time up there and getting to know the area. Shelley's advice kept coming back to her – *grab life with both hands and move on, Jess. You're a long time dead.*

When Jess arrived at the B&B she congratulated herself on driving all that way and immediately acquainted herself with the bedroom and en suite, put her feet up and made a cup of tea from the hospitality tray. Over the next few weeks she made friends with the owner and spent time scouring the estate agents and viewing properties suitable for her business. When she found Bracken Farmhouse nestling in the heart of the countryside she instantly fell in love with its old world charm, stone walls and period features. It was sadly run down but her insight told her it had potential. It would take a great deal of work to turn it into the image playing in her mind's eye but she knew at once that this was the ideal place for the next stage of her life. She toyed with the idea of asking Chris to come and take a look but in the end she wanted to do this by herself, to feel accomplished. She went with her gut instinct and put in a cheeky offer. It was accepted.

It wasn't long before she felt really comfortable in the area; it truly was like coming home. There was a stream running through the village, two pubs and a grocery store – the quintessential English village. The people were very friendly and it soon felt as if she had known them all her life. When they knew what she had planned for the old farmhouse they were all smiles and encouragement.

Having done her publicity homework Jess had put a whole page advert in the local paper three weeks prior to opening, she'd arranged a leaflet-drop around the villages and plastered the advert all across the internet. She wanted her venture to be a great success, nothing left to chance. She was determined to use the local farmers and producers too and found they all welcomed her with warm hearts and open arms, knowing they would all support each other. Jess was also hoping that the visitors to the Lakes and Peak District would pay her a visit on their way to or from their destinations.

She stood in the hallway and scanned the room next to the kitchen that had originally been the parlour. Keeping in mind all the places that had so inspired her she had decorated the room in creams and pastels with stripped pine tables and chairs. Pure white linen table cloths and white china graced the tables with the colour provided by the sweet peas taken from the garden and placed in little cut glass vases that caught the light. She had visited a local artist's exhibition the weekend after her arrival and had instantly fallen in love with her floral watercolours and commissioned her to paint some for her tea room. These now adorned the pale walls. She decided against curtains and instead had refurbished and reinstalled the original shutters at the tall windows.

Satisfied with her efforts, Jess walked into the large room the other side of the wide, high-ceilinged hall. This half of the enterprise was laid out with easy chairs and country furnishings to encourage customers to browse the locally-sourced small pieces of furniture, the delicate table lamps and homemade preserves, all artistically arranged.

Opening the stained glass and panelled front door she stood on the stone step breathing in the fresh air and felt the warm morning sun on her face and the anticipation of yet another balmy day. In the front garden, sheltered by the old stone walls, cottage garden plants and ferns were enjoying a growth spurt. Not wanting a pristine look, Jess encouraged the moss and mind-your-own-business to grow between the cobbles and the flag stones. In a reclamation yard she had found some small antique statues to place amongst the shrubbery and remembering the garden at Twin Oaks, had filled two large urns with purple pansies and placed one at each side of the front door. She went round to the back garden and took out from the shed two sets of metal tables and chairs painted in ice cream colours and arranged them in the front garden. She intended the large back garden to be her private sanctuary which she hoped to plan at a later stage.

Walking back to the kitchen she glanced at the old school clock and switched on the coffee maker. The unfitted country kitchen was one of the first things to be installed and every time she ran her hands over the distressed buttermilk finish a big smile spread across her face.

Jess had great aspirations for 'Jessica's Parlour'. She was looking forward to welcoming customers to her tea room where they could enjoy her homemade cakes, scones and light lunches, speciality teas and coffees. There were also some outbuildings that could be converted into holiday cottages at a later date and the plans for these stood on the kitchen table awaiting the final touches. There was no limit to her enthusiasm.

She set two cups and saucers on the huge pine table with a pot of freshly brewed coffee and some of her fruit scones straight from the Aga. She heard a car draw up, footsteps entering the hall and some whistling.

'Hello, love. Well, that's all sorted – the photographer from the local paper's coming tomorrow to do the feature.'

'Awesome!'

'So are you.' Eddie dropped his car keys in the dish on the dresser, sat down at the table next to Jess and planted a kiss on her lips. He picked up her hand and kissed it. 'I noticed you put some tables and chairs outside – you should've let me do that. You feeling OK?'

She nodded and smiled at him.

'Can't be too careful, you know.'

'Oh, Eddie, I'm fine. You worry too much.'

He placed a hand carefully on her tummy and she glowed, confident in her decision to make a new life with Eddie. She leant across and poured him a cup of coffee. He buttered a scone and took a mouthful devouring it hungrily. 'Mm, these are good. Big day tomorrow, then?'

'Yeah, I've arranged for us to have a big splash in *Yorkshire Life*, too. They're coming to do a feature on Jessica's Parlour next week.' She had another thought, one that had been at the back of her mind during the restoration of Bracken Farmhouse. 'What do you think Walter would've made of me spending his money on this place?'

'He'd be very proud of his great-granddaughter and so am I. It'll be great, just you wait and see,' he winked at her. 'I'll help you all I can, you know that. We've come a long way since you first told me about the will, but this is only the beginning.'

'It'll be great to see Mandy, Trevor and the twins. Becks sent me an email – she wants to poke her nose round the door, too.'

'Fantastic, the more the merrier. Sure you're up to it?'

Jess nodded and beamed at him.

After Eddie had left on the Monday night before the day of the document signing, Jess had been on the verge of calling him back. Eddie's touch had stirred something within her and she realised Giles would never feature strongly in her life. Finding him had been the start of the means to an end and she was grateful, but that was as far it went. She also realised how blinkered she'd been up till then, her one train of thought to become a rich woman no matter how she achieved it. That night after Eddie had gone home, she lay in bed unable to sleep for her mind whirling and slotting the pieces of the jigsaw together.

The following evening, Eddie wiped his sweaty palms and bit his lip as he rang Jess's door bell. It had taken him an hour to get his hands clean and another hour deciding what to wear for their evening out. Jess had on her skimpy pale blue dress and when she opened the door to him his heart turned over.

'What's the matter? Do I look all right?' she asked, her arms stuck out in a pose.

He moved closer. 'Oh, Jess. You look more than all right...' He had kissed her sensuously on the lips and he knew that, whatever happened, this moment would stay with him forever. There was a delicious aroma wafting from upstairs; Eddie looked past her, sniffing the air. 'What can I smell?'

'I've made your favourite; steak and kidney pie!'

'But...I thought we were going out?'

Eddie eagerly followed her upstairs and into the kitchenette. She went to the fridge and poured him a beer.

He smiled and shook his head. 'You never cease to amaze me. Come here.' He pulled her towards him.

She draped her arms round his neck. 'You don't mind, do you?'

'Mind? Of course I don't mind; it's just...I thought that's what you wanted – posh nosh and all that.'

Jess's mind went back to the Terrace restaurant, Giles's moods and her sore feet under the table and said, 'I thought I did, too, but you can't relax in those places.'

Eddie laughed. 'Yeah. We'd get thrown out for what I'm about to suggest!'

She slapped him playfully on the shoulder. 'Eddie! What're you like?'

He said nothing but tilted her face up to his and gave her a long lingering kiss and she moulded into him. 'Oh, Jess. You don't know how long I've wanted to do that.'

'You're right. We'd have been asked to get a room!'

During their meal, which Eddie lapped up and described as 'good-down-to-earth-grub and none of your pretty-pictures-stuff', Jess had told him of her plans for the business she hoped to open in the Dales. Eddie couldn't believe what he was hearing; at long last all his hopes and dreams were beginning to materialise, too. They had discussed the enterprise long into the night and she was surprised and excited when he told her he would draw up a business plan and that he'd been to evening classes hoping to put his knowledge to good use one day. He also told her he would give her his full backing, something Giles would never have done. Jess had never realised the opportunity to go to his boathouse but instinct told her that if she had, there would have been some serious misgivings on her part. No, she was happy to let Shelley have him. She'd be able to put him in his place and from what Shelley had told her, she never wanted to be tied down with kids. Maybe a pair well-matched on that score, and yachts, of course.

Eddie had brought her back from her thoughts. 'Penny for 'em '.

'Oh, I was just thinking about Giles and Shelley.'

'No regrets?'

Her smile sent a warm glow running through his veins. 'Nope, no regrets.'

Jess told him how she had felt that day he helped her move. 'I'm so sorry for all that I put you through, Eddie. I'll make it up to you, I promise.'

'Don't worry. We're well on the way.' He picked up her hand and kissed it. 'I always knew we'd make it, you just needed a bit of convincing.'

'I can't believe I've been so short-sighted.'

'You weren't short-sighted, just hoodwinked by all that glitz and glamour. I knew you'd come round in the end. I just had to be patient and hope you'd come to the same conclusion as me – that we're made for each other.'

Whilst making the coffee she had felt Eddie's warm breath on her neck. He moved her hair to one side and kissed her ear. He knew what this did to her and she turned and clung to him. He was hungry for her; he led her into the bedroom and they made love like two people who had only just discovered each other.

Jess was shaken back to the present when she heard Eddie say, 'You sure you're OK? You're very quiet.'

'Mm, I was just thinking about that Tuesday night in my apartment, the day after the document signing.' She leaned over and kissed him then she heard the rattle of the letter box. She went to pick up the post card that had fallen on the mat. The picture was one of a harbour in France, bright blue sky and colourful reflections in the water. She studied it for a while before flipping it over.

Hi, Jess.

Today - La Rochelle, tomorrow the world! Sea Witch is a dream. Giles sends his love. Oh, I nearly forgot. Good luck with the Grand Opening! I'll be thinking of you.

Heaps of love, Shelley. xxx

31526843R00110

Printed in Poland
by Amazon Fulfillment
Poland Sp. z o.o., Wrocław